SARA'S VOW

by
Bobbi Hitchcock

PublishAmerica
Baltimore

©2008 by Bobbi Hitchcock.
All rights reserved. No part of this book may be reproduced, stored in a retrieval system or transmitted in any form or by any means without the prior written permission of the publishers, except by a reviewer who may quote brief passages in a review to be printed in a newspaper, magazine or journal.

First printing

All characters in this book are fictitious, and any resemblance to real persons, living or dead, is coincidental.

PublishAmerica has allowed this work to remain exactly as the author intended, verbatim, without editorial input.

ISBN: 1-60474-101-5
PUBLISHED BY PUBLISHAMERICA, LLLP
www.publishamerica.com
Baltimore

Printed in the United States of America

Introduction

Parents try to teach what their children will need to know in life. They teach these life lessons as they come, believing that by the time their children are grown they can face the world. What if their time line is not the way it is going to be? Who teaches them how to face the unthinkable? When do they learn inner strength and how to push on, against all odds? Where do they turn if your not there?

In the beautiful valley of southwest Virginia, flows a shallow creek that winds and turns, offering a cool drink to any animal or human that cares to taste. As we come around a bend of trees into the valley, Papa, John Holbrook, says he can see himself raising our family here. He drives the mules, which is pulling the covered wagon, along beside the gently flowing creek. He tells us what his imagination allows him to see into our future. He says he can see his children playing in that creek. He could almost hear our squeals and laughter. Only right now I am the only child.

Crossing the creek, he pulls the wagon to a stop. I quickly poke my head out of the wagon, between him and Momma.

"Are we here now Papa?"

I am almost six and Papa says I am the kindest, most gentle soul he has ever known. He says I take it from Momma. Momma, he calls her Ruth, is a most forgiving person; and Lord knows he has given her many things to forgive, like taking her away from her family back in the old country, to move to the new world, in hopes of a better future for us. Then we had to move on, leaving the ocean side and the heavy rains and storms that rips the roofs off the houses and floods the whole area, making it impossible to get to town for food. When he heard of a wagon train going southwest, he knew this might be his last chance before he loses a member of our family to those horrid storms.

"Yes, Sara. Let me stop the mules and we will pick out where we are going to build our cabin. I want everyone to have a say. It is going to be our home, ya know." He helps Momma down and then picks me up and swings me over his head, around before putting me on the ground. I squeal with laughter. His good mood is catching and Momma laughs as she tries to protect me from falling when he sets me down. He turns the mules loose and unties the cow so they may wonder around and eat as they pleased and drink fresh water from the creek. The cow has a young heifer calf by her side that follows at her mother's heels.

Papa draws in the sand how Momma wants the house to look and then we will all work to make the picture become real.

Momma picks out a tree up on the hill, for her and me to sit under and read the Bible. I can learn to read my letters and sounds and numbers, and make my marks in the dirt. The excitement is overwhelming. We made the long trip safely, bought the land, and now we are seeing it for the first time. Plus, Momma has a secret she has not told Papa yet. There will be a new member of the family before the winter snows. Papa immediately sets up a campsite for our family. He unloads the wagon and uses the canopy to cover our things, to protect them from the weather. Momma makes our beds under the wagon for tonight.

Once that is done, he begins marking where the corners of the cabin will be.

We all help load the flat stones from the creek, on the wagon and the mules pull it up to the area where Papa starts to build the supports for the walls of the cabin. Then he falls trees to make the logs.

He clears ten trees, a number he mentally sets for a goal, then trims off the limbs and stacks them in a pile for later, we want a porch to sit on in the evenings and enjoy the sites and time with family and someday friends. Then he takes the mules, hitching the mules to the logs. Next he has them drag the logs to the cabin spot, where he unhitches the mules and goes back for more logs. The process starts all over again. Each time he placing the logs where they will be used to build the walls, making sure he has enough for the height and length of each wall.

Soon he has enough to build the walls. The front and back are going to be longer than the sides so he has to use the longer logs there.

The mules drag them to the area one by one. He makes straight lines in the dirt, and asks Momma if that is big enough or if she wants it bigger. He walks it toe to heel on all four sides to be sure it is the same length in front as in back and the sides are the same size.

The steps are logs split in half and the rails across the front porch are limbs from the trees. Papa doesn't believe in wasting anything. He leaves long window holes in the walls and say's someday he would order some of the fancy glass they have back east to put in them.

I join my parents in pushing the logs into place. Papa has to have them be lined up just right. I talk and grunt while I push. Building a house is a great adventure for me, because I was never big enough to help before when a house was to be built, back east.

The men did the work and women made sure they had plenty of water to drink and everyone pitched in and they all ate together. The women would set the tables and the men would come and eat. The children were fed when the women ate. I miss all my friends.

Now, it is just the three of us. I realize I am not only a part of the family but now I feel almost like a grownup. I must work very hard to prove I am worthy.

As I push, my feet slip in the dirt and I must bring my feet back where they belong. My knees buckle and I fall but I keep my hands on the logs and keep pushing. I don't want to look too weak and small that Papa will make me stop. Sometimes, he is just too over protective of me. I am a big girl now and wish to prove it to him. Maybe, he will let me help build the barn and stalls.

Within a week the walls are standing and all that is left is the roof. Papa trims the long narrow limbs and then ties a rope on one end. Taking the rope, he climbs a ladder onto the roof and Momma and I help by pushing the limbs up to him from below. He ties the limbs down going from top to bottom first. Next he ties the limbs going crossways, to the limbs already tied down. He puts them as close to each other as he can, tightening the open areas.

He stands up every now and then, bending backwards, to straighten the tighten muscles. His back is hurting something awful, but at least the hardest work is done. Now tomorrow all he has to do is pack the open areas so the weather will not come into the house below.

Once the roof is completed, Papa begins to make shutters for the windows to keep out the cold winds and rain. Using something he calls a plane, he shears off the bark, and makes planks. Using the planks, the shutters are done. The front has a window for the kitchen area, one for the area by the bed, the kitchen has a second one on the side of the house and there is one on the back of the house that will face where the stalls and barn will be built one day soon.

We decide we want a rock fireplace in the back of the house, so the rocks that Momma and I gather while Papa was making the shutters, are in a pile and just waiting for Papa to bring the wagon over to haul them to the house. Now my back hurts too. Momma doesn't complain but I see her stretching this way and that way to loosen the tight muscles too.

I talk about each rock, telling Papa exactly where we found it, as I bring the heavy rocks to be put on the fireplace chimney. He admires each one and smiles as I spin around to go back to fetch another one. Momma is silently laughing and when Papa sees her grinning, it makes him laugh too. There is nothing better then making my parents laugh.

He has loved Momma since they were children. There never was another woman that interested him, and it was the same for her. Their parents were close and they lived in the same village, attended the same church and school. It was no surprise they married.

SARA'S VOW

When I grow up I want it to be the same way for me, too.

Papa builds the fireplace in three days. As I give him each stone, I show him where I think he should place it. Then I step back and look at it and say: "Yes, Papa, there looks just right. Now lets do the next one." Papa laughs as he bends down to pick up more mud.

Papa packs each space with a chunk of thick mud and smoothes it over the edges of the rocks. The mud helps keep the rocks in place and the winds and rain from blowing in. Momma is busy mixing the mud and grasses to be sure it is not too wet or too dry. The mud has grasses for fillers to make it hold in place and turn rock hard.

Finally, the house is built and together we stand outside and look at it. Papa still needs to add on the porch and the railings, but we can move in now.

As we stand outside, Papa picks me up in his arms, moving me to one side and resting me on his left hip; taking Momma's hand they bow their heads and ask for God to bless our home.

We immediately begin to carry in our belongings to fill the cabin. Tonight we will sleep in our beds, in our new home. Excitement is in the air. Tired, we laugh and giggle a lot.

Tomorrow, Papa will dig the well and we will not have to fetch water from the creek anymore. The water is good, but having the well close by will be much better.

Momma's belly has really gotten big and there is no hiding that a baby would be coming.

Secretly I wish for it to be a girl, I would love a sister to play with, but a brother would be ok too, he can help Papa and me with the work outside.

I watch, from up on the hill, Papa digging the well. I wish I could go down and help him but Momma wants me to start back on my reading and writing. We sit under the tree and I make my marks in the sand. The shade of the tree keeps us from getting too hot. Momma can't tolerate the heat much anymore now the baby is growing so fast.

Once the well is finished, Papa and I start on the barn and corral.

It takes a lot of trees and limbs to build a barn and corral, but the mules work hard and soon they have a home of their own.

The sun cast it's warming rays down on my shining face, as I watch my Papa work the two mules pulling up the tree stumps with ropes. The mules pull and tug at the ropes that are fasten to them while my Papa guides them with the other end of the ropes from one side to the other, never raising his voice but offering encouragement and orders. I swing my small body side to side as if trying to help the mules pull.

Every morning for a week now I sit on the same step and watch my father. I am amazed at his determination to get the field done and at the same time making sure he does not push the mules too hard, that they have time to rest and cool off before they get a drink from the well water. I learn a lot from watching and listening.

I see Papa as a giant of a man. He is the strongest person I have ever met. He is firm, however, most of the time I see the tender side of him, like how his eyes glow with the love he has for Momma and me. He takes on a funny look when he watches Momma mend or clean. I have also caught him watching me play, with a smile on his face and that same funny expression. It always makes me smile back and wave. I remember how the people on the wagon train listened to him, never knowing if it was his size, or tone of voice that made people just want to follow him and do what he said. What ever it was, everyone made it through those mountain passes and settled here. Surrounded by tall mountains and forest full of animals, I cannot imagine a better place to live. It is perfect.

He shows me leaves to use for healing wounds and what leaves would make me itch. Vines with thorns and vines that would bare grapes and berries, however, I need to understand this is also where bears would be to wanting to eat the berries too, so to keep my ears and eyes open, watching all directions. There could snakes also under those bushes and vines so I have to keep my eyes open and always watching.

I am so deep in thought I almost miss hearing Momma call me from inside the house.

Jumping up quickly, I rush through the door, and see my mother still in bed. Stopping, with a frown on my face, I slowly walk over to the bedside and touch my mothers face. She is cool but sweat beads are rolling down her cheeks.

"You OK Momma? Is there anything I can get you? Is it the baby?"

"Yes, Sara I am just fine. I think it is time for the baby to come. I need you to go out and get Papa and tell him to come on in now. Can you do that for me Sweetie?" She brushes hair from my face and tries to give me an encouraging smile.

"Ya think the baby's time to be born is come?" I could hardly keep the excitement out of my voice. I have waited so long for this moment.

"Yes, and I need your father. Can you go and get him for me?" She speaks softly. I have never heard her raise her voice except to call Papa in from the fields to eat, or me from the creek.

I didn't wait to answer but as I run out the front door I yell back; "I will have him back here before you can say jumping frog legs."

I run across the plank porch and jump over the steps and although I almost fall, I keep on running and begin to call my father, long before he can hear me. I don't care; I just keep on calling him and never taking my eyes off of him or the mules.

"Papa, Papa, the baby is coming…Papa, Papa, the baby is coming!" With the running and yelling at the top of my lungs; I become winded and my lungs feel like they are going to burst, I am dizzy and try hard not to fall.

Just as I gets close, he hears me, however, the harder I try I am having a hard time getting any words out. He sees me as I double over trying to get my breath. I point toward the house and get out "Momma says baby…" and he understands and throws down the reins and starts running for the house. I smile as I see him running across the fresh plowed earth, then sit down, trying to catch my breath.

I reach over and take the reins. Papa forgot to unhitch the mules. I smile. I have seen him do it many times, then without another thought, decide surely I can do it. After all it can't be all that hard. Common sense tells me I have also never walked the mules back to their stalls by myself; but on the other hand there is a first time for everything. My mind is made up and I know what I need to do. Won't Papa be surprised when he sees what I did for him? He is always doing things for others and never asks for anything himself. I grin with the surprise I am going to do for Papa. Now if the mules will just behave, I will give them fresh water and pull some grass for them.

Looking at how far away the barn is, and feeling some fear, I worry what if they break loose and run away? How will I find them in the woods? What if I can't find them before dark? After all Papa didn't tell me to put them up. How long does it take to have a baby anyway? Would he be back in a couple of minutes or would it be an hour?

As I relax from my dash across the field, my breathing returns to normal again. I stand up and look toward the house. I listen really hard and didn't hear the baby crying yet. Thinking out loud, I begin to talk to myself.

"Well, I am just going to have to put the mules up. They cooled off by now and it will be all right for them to have some water and I can pull up some green grass as a reward for behaving. Papa always says we got to take care of the animals because they take care of us. I guess that means me too."

I pick up the reins, and look at the mules that tower over me. Either one could walk away and drag me with them. How am I going to get them to follow me back?

Putting my hands on my hips, I spread my legs, just a bit, to take a stance. I hope it will let them know I mean business and they better listen to me.

"Okay, This is what I am going to do. See, I am going to walk you to the well and get cha some water. Then we are going to walk to the barn and I will get cha some grass. This is what you're going to do.

SARA'S VOW

You are going to behave yourselves and walk really slow with me. See Papa is in the house with Momma making a baby be born. So, you can behave and get water and something to eat or you can stay out here all night." Putting my thumb against my chest, I continue: "If I were you, I would rather be in the barn. So we got a deal?"

I wait for an answer. Something to let me know they understood me.

Sally, the lead mule, begins to walk towards the house. I quickly grab the reins and get in front of her. Clyde, the other mule, follows slightly behind Sally.

"I thought you would see to my way of thinking. Won't Papa be surprised when he comes out and your all fed and watered and in your stalls? Maybe he will think I am big enough to go hunting now. Wouldn't that be just about the best thing ever? Momma wouldn't be alone because she would have the baby and Papa and I can go hunting by ourselves. Maybe I can get me a bear and Papa can help me save the hide and I can make Momma a rug for the house. The baby can sleep on it and stay warm. Yep, I think that's a swell idea I just had." I smile real big as I march the mules toward the water well, just outside the kitchen window, on the south side of the cabin.

The mules stop at the well, waiting for their drink of water before heading on to the barn.

I drop the bucket down into the well, but hang onto the rope to be sure I can get the bucket back up the well. I listen and hear the splash, I lean over and check but the bucket is still right side up, so I jerk the rope several times and it finally tips over and sinks as it fills with water.

"There that wasn't so hard." I start to pull the bucket back up. Only the higher the bucket gets the harder it is to pull up, even with the pulley Papa had made out of a broken wagon wheel hub. Soon I am huffing and puffing and the rope is slipping through my small hands. I sit down on the ground and pull and the rope still slides back out of my hands. I put my feet against the well and then lay back and pull with all my might. Each time I let go with one hand to get a higher grip the rope slips through and I am losing some of the length I had gained, but I refuse to give up. Papa and Momma never give up, neither will I.

Finally, I stand back up and start spinning around and around; wrapping the rope around my waist and the bucket comes higher and higher. Soon the rope is wrapped from my chest to my hips and the bucket is still in the well, so I sit back down and the bucket comes all the way out. Now all I have to figure how to keep the bucket up while I stand up and unwrap myself.

Molly, not understanding why it is taking so long to get them their water, walks around the well to where I am sitting looking up at the rope. Sally sniffs my hair, and then she steps forward. As luck would have it, she is standing on the rope and I immediately know I have to get up fast before Sally steps back off the rope and the bucket drops back into the well. Sally stands still, watching me as I grab the bucket and slide it over the rock wall that was built around the well hole. The rope is getting tighter as I move to get the bucket on the ground, but I bear the uncomfortable tightness to keep Sally on the rope as I strain to get the bucket on the ground.

As Sally drinks, I wiggle out of the rope and get Clyde to move around to this side of the well and get a drink also. Standing there, watching the mules drink, I feel very proud of myself. I may only be six years old but I just did a grownup's chore without any help and that made me feel down right big.

As the mules drink their water, I untangle their ropes and disconnect them from their halters. Using just the reins I take one in each hand and lead them to the stalls. Once they are inside, I give them both several armfuls of grass I pull up by hand. Standing back, I watch them eat and feel the sting on my fingers from pulling all that grass. I see where I had rubbed blisters and then tore the skin off of them. They burned but nothing I can't bare.

"Ya know, Papa is going to be down right proud of me when he sees what I just did all by myself. Oh sure, ya'll helped by behaving yourselves and I do appreciate that understand.

Still I think I did a fair job getting ya out of that field and back in here so ya can get a good night sleep. Now eat and then get to bed. I doubt if Papa will want to stay in the house tomorrow when there are still more stumps in the field that need tending to. So get to bed and I will see ya in the morning."

I walk back to the cabin, too tired to run, I wipe my hands on the seat of my skirt. When I step up on the porch I hear Papa call out to me.

"Sara stay outside until I tell ya it is time to come in."

I turn and sit down on the old tree stump that Papa left just for me to sit on at night. I glance back and start to remember how it was when we first came here.

The corral is made from tree limbs, some are post and the smaller ones are made into pole rails. I remember how Momma and I work to help him hold poles while he fastened them to the post for the corral and stalls. Then when he was working on the roof we would pass limbs up to him like we did with the cabin.

We work as a family, and love and worship as a family. We are the only ones in the area as far as we know. No neighbors have come by. It sure gets lonely.

My mind drifts back to the present, remembering how Papa tells funny stories to us at night and Momma and I sit by the fireplace and laugh until we cry, seeing the tears only makes us laugh harder. He gets up and tries to show us how it happened and he makes even the dullest stories funny.

As time passes and it starts to get dark, I remember back to the days of the wagon train. There were a few children on the train but only one boy who was close enough to my age to play with. He had blond hair and the prettiest blue eyes and the funniest laugh that I have ever heard. He liked me because I didn't insist on playing with dolls but liked to climb trees and big rocks and go hunting for what ever we could find on the rest breaks. I liked him because he treated me like a friend and not some sissy girl that would be afraid of bugs or scrapping a knee or elbow. I miss him most of all.

I hear my mother cry out and beg God to help make the baby come. My mother's cries scare me and I wrap my arms around my knees and put my head on them then close my eyes to pray. It is the thing to do when someone needs help, and I want HIM to help my mother and stop the pain.

Later, I get to thinking about having a baby of my own someday and now not sure if I will ever have a baby, just too darn hard to get them out of the belly! I decide that night I will just have dogs that have puppies and cats with their kittens, chickens hatching baby chicks and horses with colts and fillies. Who needs all the pain? Animals are cuter anyway.

I look up at the sky. It is so clear I can see all the millions of stars and the moon is just a sliver hanging and waiting for the new baby to be born. I stand up, looking at all the stars and turn around and around, with my arms stretched out to the sides. So many stars shining, all colors. I feel a slight breeze, and can smell the fresh turned earth from the tree stumps. What a wonderful place to be born in. It is like everything is here waiting to see the new baby.

I sit back down on the stump to wait, when I hear Papa step out on the porch. I turn and see his smile. He walks over and kneels down beside me.

"Ya have a brother. I expect ya to help teach him the things he should know, things your mother and I have long forgotten. Things like how to play and use your imagination. How to hide and be so still that even I have a hard time finding you. Do you think ya can do this?" He looks so serious, doesn't smile, so I know this is important.

"Yes, Oh Yes Papa." I am tingling all over, to be given such a responsibility.

Papa looks up at the stars and wraps his arm around me.

"The angels are coming to see your brother I see. Every star is an angel. Sometimes, I talk to my Papa. He is up there. A great man he was. I surely miss him. He passed on before we left the old country. He would have loved meeting ya. Oh how he loved the little girls and boys that came to play at his home. My own mother passed when I was just a small child. She is up there, too. When I am feeling lonely, I come out here and look up at all the angels looking down on us and I can talk to my folks anytime I want. Sure is comforting. Now, lets go and see that baby brother of yours."

Taking my hand, he leads me into the cabin.

Chapter One

Looking up into my Father's eyes I ask: "Is he all right?" Is Momma all right?"

Squeezing my hand he nods.

"He is a wee lad but he is strong. Come and see for yourself."

Together, we turn toward the bed, and I can feel me smiling from ear to ear.

I tiptoe over to the bedside, looking up at Papa, I hear him say:

"Timothy. I named him after my father and his father before him. It is a Biblical name and has been in the family for generations." His sleeves are still rolled above his elbows.

"I named him from the good book just as your mother named you. Let us kneel beside the bed and thank God for this blessing he has bestowed on our family."

As I kneel down by the bed, I take my mother's hand and reach for Papa's.

He shakes his head and gently picks up the tiny hand of Timothy and places it in my hand.

I know my face is beaming with pride, I can feel the heat and my heart is racing wild from excitement. I ask myself; "Can it ever get any better than this?"

He takes Timothy's other hand and with his other hand takes Momma's hand. As a family we thanked God for the blessings He has given us, and the addition that God has added to our family circle of praise. We just had our first prayer as a completed family.

SARA'S VOW

As I open my eyes I look into my mothers arms. Timothy is all red, his hair is wet still and yet he is the most beautiful baby I have ever seen. I had seen several when we lived in the city and then again on the wagon train, babies were being born. None, not one, is as pretty as Timothy, my brother, though.

"Momma, do you think it would be all right if I kissed my brother?" She nods and smiles.

I lean over and ever so gently kiss him on the cheek and then I start to whisper to him as I rest my body on the bed and scoot closer to his ear.

"I promise I will always take care of you. I will be there if you need to learn anything. I will teach you everything I know." Looking up at my mother, I smile.

"If you ever need help, just ask me and I will be there to help you, too, Momma."

She puts her right hand on my shoulder and tells me:

"I know you will always be here whenever I need ya. I will always need you and your Papa, and now I also have Timothy to complete our family." She smiles and closes her eyes for just a moment. She looks so tired; I scoot back off the bed as gently as I can. Papa turns and picks up his hat.

"I best get out there and put those mules up. I don't think we will be working any more tonight."

"Too late, Papa. I already did that. They have been watered and fed and they are probably sleeping by now. Don't need to go and disturb them. I did it right. Just like I seen you do many a time." It is hard keeping a straight face, with Papa's surprised look on his face, but it quickly changes into a large grin and I feel a burst of pride.

Momma smiles real big and reaches out to rub my arm as I look down at her and see her pride. It was worth all the trouble for this moment with my parents. One I shall never, ever forget.

"Your growing up so fast. I am so proud of you. Taking on that chore must have been really scary but you still did it. Your very special, did I ever tell you that? If I didn't I should have."

"Oh Momma, you tell me that all the time. But I ain't nothing special, I just did what needed to be done like you and Papa. When there is something that's needs a doing, you just do it. I have been watching you and Papa for my whole life and that's what you do. It just seems right I do it too."

Momma's eyes close and I see a tear slid down her cheek. Papa steps up and whispers it is time for everyone to get some sleep.

The next morning I wake with Timothy crying. I jump up and see that Papa is already working in the field and Momma is asleep. I walk over and look at the tiny baby. I have never changed a baby before, so I look at the detail on how Momma had put the cloth on him and get a cloth and fold it, just like Momma had shown me and I practiced all winter.

The only thing is there was no baby to practice on before. All I could do is to hope I do it right and it doesn't fall off.

Timothy's cloth is not only wet but dirty also. I get the water and put it on the fire in the fireplace. Then I gather the cloths Momma and I had cut up to make cloths for the baby. When the water is warm, I test it with my wrist and then pick up Timothy and put him carefully in the dishpan, holding his head up out of the water. I use my other hand to wash him. He is kicking and slippery and several times his head slips under the water, and he comes up coughing but doesn't cry. I take him out and dry him off, talking to him the whole time.

Once dressed I place him back in his wood crate and start to make Momma some breakfast. I gather the eggs from the basket, crack them and drop the insides gently into the hot iron frying pan on the fire. I had cooked the last of the bacon the night before and its grease is already hot and ready for the eggs. We have been out of deer meat for several weeks. Papa keeps saying he will get some more meat as soon as the field is cleared.

Momma had made plenty of biscuits, enough to last for at least a week and with fresh gravy, the eggs would be plenty.

With breakfast completed, I go to wake up Momma. Thinking she will want to get up. I lay a dress on the bed and am getting her shoes when I feel her touching my hand.

"Your growing up so fast, Sara. I can remember not long ago when you were born and you were so tiny. I was scared that I wouldn't take care of you right or that I would drop you or hurt you in some way. I watched you give your brother a bath. You didn't think twice about doing that, where did you learn such courage? That would have scared me to death when I was your age. Your such a brave little girl, and I do love you so much." She opens her arms and I immediately lie down and curl up in them. Even though it is good to feel grown up, there are times when I like to feel like a little girl sometimes.

"I am trying to be like a grown up. I want to help you and Papa as much as I can and I want to learn to take care of Timothy and play with him. I have been a little girl long enough. The way I figure it, if I learn all the hard stuff when I am just a little girl then it won't be hard when I grow up and have a baby of my own."

A week passes and I am really getting organized and able to take on more and more chores. Meals are getting easier to prepare, and the time alone with Momma and Timothy is working out great.

Now when I take Papa his meal I have the time to sit and eat with him. We talk about the fields and the mules and even trapping this winter when the furs are thickest.

While I clean the cabin Momma and I talk. We laugh and talk about my lessons up on the hill and how one day we will be teaching Timothy how to read too. We talk about the fall colors and how pretty the trees are then. Momma even talks about how grown up I am becoming. We laughed about my taking the mules and putting them up and how I got water out of the well.

"I did it all by myself, just like him, and now Papa can take me on one of the mules. I will be able to keep up. I am going to shoot you a bear and make you a rug for Timothy to play on this winter and stay warm."

"Oh My; Ya have been planning this for a long time haven't cha?"

"Sure. Sitting out on that porch gives a person a lot of time to just think about things and make plans. When I get my work done I sit out there and think about all sorts of things."

"Sometimes, things just don't work out the way we plan them. Things just don't go right and we have to change our plans and do things differently." She smiles as she remembers all the dreams she has had and how they changed as time went on. Some days she tells about those dreams. Some we laugh about and some are really nice. She does this a lot here lately.

"You trying to tell me, nicely that Papa ain't going to take me with him this winter?"

"I don't know what you and your Papa will do this winter. We don't know what will happen tomorrow. We could make plans for a picnic and it could rain. Remember all the times we went up to the tree and I taught you your letters? Remember when the wet weather came we had to stay inside by the fire to learn them? Only God knows what will happen tomorrow. We don't give up. When times get hard we have to try harder to make sure they are right. I want you to promise me, if times get bad that you will always take good care of your little brother and never, ever give up."

I realize this is something really important stand up and lock fingers with my mother. Looking at Momma in the eye, I hold my head up high and stick my chin out...

"I, Sara Holbrook, do make this vow to my mother...no matter what, I will take care of my brother, we are one blood, we are family."

Smiling, Momma lays her head back and relaxes.

"Your so grown up. This is not a game. A vow is more than a promise; you must do everything to keep it. When Papa and I got married, we made a vow to love each other until death parts us, and even then we will continue to love the other."

"When I grow up, I want to find someone just like Papa for me to make a vow like that with." I wonder if I will even meet someone way out here.

"Then I will pray you find you such a man, but that will be years from now. So don't go looking for no man to marry any time soon, ya hear?"

"Momma, there ain't even any boys around here. I really don't think you need to worry about that. Besides, I don't like boys, except for Timothy."

"You use to play with that little blond headed boy on the wagon train, remember?"

"Oh sure. The girls, all they wanted to do was play with dolls. They didn't want to go and catch frogs or snakes or anything fun. Johnny and I did all kinds of fun things."

"Your not responsible for the snake in the Captains wagon are you? Never mind I don't want to know." Laughing she stares at me, like she can see into my mind and know the truth.

"If I tell you will I get into trouble?" Laughing, but with a suspicious look on my face.

"No, but I don't think I want to know any more." Giggling she knows I did it; she waves her hand back and forth.

She takes me in her arms and holds me tight for a while. She says we are so much alike. She drifts off with memories of her own wild stunts probably, because she was smiling.

When I hear my mother's deep steady breathing I get up and return to my work, smiling and wondering what my future holds for me and wonder if Momma will ever tell me about what she did.

Chapter Two

I get up before the sun, and start the fire for Papa's breakfast. As soon as he eats he heads straight for the field. He works until dusk every day.

I begin by gathering eggs and giving the chickens fresh water. I water the few wild flowers that Momma and I planted during the summer when we built the cabin. Sometimes I pick a few and put them in water for her, before I come in and start to prepare breakfast for Momma and me.

As soon as breakfast is finished I clean the kitchen and start cooking for dinner, this I will take to the field at noon to feed Papa, and we sit and talk until he has to go back to work.

There is a big tree we sometimes sit under and he keeps his water under it to keep cool. He promised to never cut this tree down, for it is our special tree. Soon it will be Timothy's special tree too. Actually, it is five trees that grew so close together that their trunks are as one but further up the trunks separate into different trees again. It makes a great hollow place to put the water, to keep it cool. The limbs and branches stretch out in all directions and then come back to touch the ground. We have to crawl under to get to the shade. It stays cool; under there, and with very little sunshine the weeds can't grow. Only the leaves when they fall make the ground like a soft bed.

Next on schedule will be Timothy's bath and then he sleeps with Momma in bed, while I sweep the cabin and wipe everything off. Sometimes I throw the dishwater on the wood plank floors on the porch to wash it off. That way we don't track in dirt from outside.

SARA'S VOW

Once the house is clean, I relax with Momma on the bed while we study my lessons or just talk. This is our special time together. Timothy is always sleeping and I enjoy this private time with just the two of us. I want to be just like Momma when I grow up.

Bright sunny mornings I rush through my inside chores so I can do the washing. I have to do the cloths for Timothy and some of Papa's shirts this morning.

Papa strung a line across from the water well to a tall tree limb for laundry to dry. It is tall enough for the mules to walk under. From the tree it slopes down to the top of the well.

I have to stand on the upside down bucket to reach the line, to hang up the clothes. I pick up a shirt and grab for the line as I step up on the bucket and then steady myself, then quickly fold it over the line before I fall off the unsteady bucket. Then I get down and pick up something else to hang up and do it all over again.

I am bringing in the clean dry clothes, with my nose stuck in them, to show Momma how much better they smell from being washed and hung out in the fresh air to dry. In wet weather we have to hang them all around the inside of the cabin. Then they take on a smoke smell. I think they smell nice but now the fresh smell smells better. Cleaner smell.

I walk through the cabin door, I see Momma lying in a blood soaked bed.

In a weaken voice Momma says: "Sara, please bring me Timothy."

I pick him up from a sound sleep and gently put him into her arms. I turn to go and get Papa but Momma stops me.

"I need this time with you and Timothy. I will be going away soon and I need you to promise me that you will take care of him. Promise you will keep him near you at all times and help Papa teach him Gods laws. Promise me you will never forget that you are family; you are one blood. Papa will teach him how to be a great man and a caring father and husband. He will help you study the Bible and teach Timothy."

A sharp pain hits and I see the pain on my mother's face and watch as her body tightens.

"Momma? Is there something I can do for you or get for you?"

Worry is seen in the frown on my face and the fear in my eyes, and this is the last thing my mother wants right now. I am not to be frightened. She knows she must remain calm for me. I try my best to look brave but I know I can't fool her.

I try not to look worried or scared with a smile.

"I think I need Papa. Can you please go to the field and fetch him for me. Tell him to come quick now, ya hear?" Words are spoken softly and a little faster than what Momma usually speaks.

"I promise Momma. Please, Momma, I am scared. Don't go away Momma!" I turn quickly and dash out the door, shouting:

"We will be right back, Momma."

Tears running down my cheeks, I clear the porch steps in one jump and keep on running. I fall a couple of times due to the soft dirt, but get back up and start running again. Something is wrong, very wrong and I know it with every breath I take. I can sense that it is important for Papa to be with Momma right now. Time is important. Although my feet keep betraying me and I fall down, skinning my knees on tree roots or pieces of stumps, I just get up and start running again. Nothing can stop me from getting to Papa, nothing!

Papa sees me running towards him and stops the mules and ties them to the plow.

Finally, reaching Papa, I am gasping for air. I try to get my breath but my heart is pumping so fast that I hear it pounding in my ears and just can't seem to make my chest take in air.

"Why are you crying, Child?" Papa steps towards me and takes me by my shoulders; holding onto my shoulders, fear makes him grab me tight, too tight, by the shoulders and it hurts, but I know he doesn't mean to hurt me.

He knows something terrible has had to happen.

"Papa, Momma wants you to come quickly." The tears flowing down my cheeks.

SARA'S VOW

I watch, as Papa doesn't stop to talk, to hug me, or to wipe away the tears. He takes off running, like a bear is after him. He runs back to the cabin; exactly what I expected him to do. Momma needs him.

I sit and catch my breath then I get up and walk slowly back the house, crying and praying, refusing to think what could be happening.

"Please God help my Momma, don't let her be in pain. Make her all better again."

When I reach the porch, I sit down on the steps and wait. I want to go in but just can't stand to see my mother in pain and crying. I hear crying. At first I think it is Papa but he never cries so it has to be Momma, I know it is not Timothy.

The sun is high when Papa comes out and tells me that Momma wishes to see me.

I am so afraid but can't understand why. I hold up my head and whisper to myself that I am a big girl now.

"If I can draw water and put the mules away I can go in and be with Momma without crying like some baby. Timothy is the baby of the house now and I going to teach him how to play and to climb a tree and not use the cloths but to water the trees and use the outhouse Papa has built."

So, I will walk into the cabin with my head held high and smile for my mother.

"Come and lay with me." Momma's words are soft and barely above a whisper.

She wraps her arms around me. I turn and smell her hair. I never want to leave this spot again. As long as I lay here Momma will be all right. I am going to will it to be so. I close my eyes and think really hard that what ever is wrong will heal.

"Sometimes in life we must face hardships that we really don't want to face." Momma's voice is soft.

"Like the move from the ocean to here?" I am determined not to let this to get hard.

"Well, maybe. Thing is, when we face hard times, we don't know it but it makes us stronger. The little things don't seem so hard any more."

"Like my taking the mules to the barn by myself?" Keep the conversation fun Sara, I tell myself.

"Yes. You did what you had to do and faced your fears and now don't you feel stronger for it?" Her voice is weak but I can hear the pride in it.

She hugs me gently and kisses me lightly on my head, but I cannot make myself look up at her, if I do, I will see in her eyes what she is trying to tell me and I don't want to hear it, not now, not ever!

"It is important, Sara, to learn about being family and sticking together and the love you have for one another that will never die." She gently takes my index finger and folds it around her index finger and says: "I want you to remember this sign; and use it when you feel sad. It will help make you strong in the hard times that life brings. Things change in our lives, and sometimes they are good and sometimes they are not so good."

Now I understand, she is making me listen so I can.

Momma is going to go away and she is not going to take Timothy or me with her. I saw this on the wagon train, but never thought it would happen to us. My life is about to change forever and so is my brother's. What will Papa do without Momma?

"NO, I don't want things to change. I am happy here. We are all happy."

I can't look at her. I look out the window and up to the sky. I don't want her to see my tears or my fears. I want to be brave. I know deep inside my mother has no choice, but it does not make the pain I am feeling any less.

Papa comes over and lays Timothy in his mother's arms. He kneels down by the bed and takes her other hand and begins to pray.

"NO, stop it Papa, don't give up. We have to do something to save Momma." I turn and run out the door, clear the porch steps and run up to the tree on the hill, where Momma has been teaching me to read the Bible. It is our special place, sometimes we had picnics up there and sometimes I took naps up there with my mother reading to me.

"It is our special place." I cry out.

Dropping to my knees, I go to the one person that can save Momma.

"Please God, Don't take my Momma. My heart is breaking and I know I have no say. Please don't take her. I still need her and so does Timothy and Papa."

I open my eyes and look up at the clouds and then look all around.

"I am all alone, all I see is dead trees and stumps, uprooted from their homes. Their lives are changed forever, and now mine is going to change, too."

Then I remember my promise and Timothy. I force myself to stand up and taking one step at a time, I slowly walk back to the cabin. A heavy weight seems to weigh me down with each step but I tighten my jaws and make fists with both hands, and hold my head up high.

"I may have to live with changes in my life, but there is not anything I can't do with Papa's help and teaching. I have to be strong. I have a baby to take care of. I promised."

When I get back to the cabin, I slowly and as silently as I can, walk to the door and peek in, then stop, as chills run up and down my back.

Papa is sitting beside Momma holding her hand to his cheek. He is crying. I have never seen Papa cry before and it is scary. I softly take another step closer.

There seems to be darkness in the room now. I strain my eyes to see, and find Timothy is still lying in Momma's arms. Papa reaches up and with his hand and he closes Momma's eyes. Then he picks up her hand and kisses it and holds it against his cheek, again.

I understand what is happening, walking over to the bed, I pick up Timothy and put him back in his wooden crate. Then, I walk outside to the well and bring up the milk.

For the longest I just look at the bucket of milk and think about the cow. She is still alive and so is her baby. I feel jealous. I don't want them to die but I want my Momma too.

Then without thinking, I return to inside the cabin, walk to the sink and prepare my brother a cup of milk. Not a sound do I make.

I pick up Timothy, and step outside. Sitting on the steps I drop spoons of milk into his mouth. When he goes to sleep I look out at the field in front of me. Not once do I look down at the baby in my arms. Not once do I speak to him or shed a tear. I feel nothing. I don't even have any thoughts, or notice if there is a breeze or not.

"We keep the meat and milk in separate buckets to keep them cool. This will make it last longer. The other way we keep meat is to dry it in strips and Papa uses this meat when he is hunting. It is very chewy and it makes the mouth water. We learned this after we came to this country. We had to learn a whole new way of living for over here.

Do you remember the Indians who met the wagon train and they had nice things made of shells and wood? Well, they also had this meat and one of the women told me how they made it. I traded some bread I had just made for the meat. Papa couldn't stop tasting it. Momma laughs.

"I really enjoy pleasing Papa and he is sometimes like a kid when he gets something new."

I look around. I could swear I just heard Momma talking to me. Momma is nowhere to be seen. She is gone. I look around and then pick up the meat. I know I heard Momma talking but I also know Momma is gone forever now. She can't be talking to me.

I return to the cabin and see Papa wrapping Momma up in the cover on the bed. He slowly lifts her up into his arms and carries her out of the cabin. He carefully lays her in the back of the buckboard. Then he walks around back to get the pick and shovel. He puts them next to Momma. Next, he walks to the field to get the mules. When he comes back, he gently backs them up and hooks them to the buckboard.

I stand in front of the window watching, understanding he is going to bury her and I wonder where. I saw people die on the wagon train and how the men buried them on the trail. Momma has gone to live with Jesus and has left Timothy and me behind with Papa.

Papa comes in later and tells me to get Timothy and together we walk up the hill to Momma's favorite tree. It is the big oak that she loved to sit under and read the Bible. The same place we sat while I learned my sounds and words from the Bible. Momma said it was important for a lady to be educated in these times.

"Who will teach me now?" I wonder as I walk behind the buckboard with Timothy in my arms. I didn't want to ride. If I did, I would never enjoy riding in a buckboard again. I would always remember how it was Momma's last ride to the hill.

Papa digs a deep hole, while Timothy and me stand by watching. I remember back in the big city that they buried people in boxes, and on the trail sometimes they were buried in gun boxes. When the gun boxes were all used up they buried them wrapped up like Momma, and just put them in the deep hole.

"How Momma is going to get out to become an angel or a star in the sky?"

Papa stops and wipes the sweat from his forehead.

"Momma is already gone. Her spirit leaves the minute she stops breathing. This is just the body she used while she was here with us. Momma is already watching us from heaven."

I look up and wave to her. "Hi Momma, Can you see us?"

Papa smiles. Then he steps out of the hole. He comes over to Timothy and me and kneels down and puts his arms around us.

"Yes, she sees both of you. She can see me too. She knows we love her and already miss her and that one-day we will be with her again.

She will be waiting for us when our time comes. She will be just as pretty as she was here and we will recognize her the minute we see her. Momma is not weak anymore and she does not feel pain. We should be happy for her."

"Oh Papa. I will be happy for her but I will be very unhappy for us. What are we going to do without Momma?" Tears began to fill my eyes but Papa wipes them away.

"We will be fine. I am here to take care of ya and you are such a big girl, ya already know how to take care of Timothy. We are still family and we will continue as one. Don't cha worry about us. We will be fine." He kisses me on the cheek and wiggles Timothy's hand.

Papa turns and goes to the buckboard. He gently picks up Momma carefully carries her to the grave. He holds onto her for a few minutes then he bends down and lowers her into the grave.

As Papa starts to shovel in the dirt, I start to shout.

"Please Papa. Don't cover her just yet. Please let her be with us a little longer. I am not ready to say goodbye, Papa. Timothy doesn't even know her yet. Oh Papa what are we going to do without Momma?" Tears flowing down my cheeks, blinding me. I hold Timothy all the tighter to my chest. Then both of us are being held next to Papa's chest and together we cry.

I watch as Papa buries Momma. Once I could no longer see any cloth, I feel stronger and am able to watch without the tears. My head high, I look up and smile at the stars as they are starting to come out.

Days past and I do both my chores and Papa's. He sits up on the hill by the grave during the day and comes in at night. I move Timothy next to my bed so I can take care of him better. Timothy cries a lot and I don't want him to bother Papa.

One night, I hear him talking out on the stump. I realize he is talking to Momma.

"Ruth, I am going to have to take the children back east. This wilderness is too wild for them. I need help raising them. I just can't take care of them like I should and still work the fields and hunt. I am just too scared to leave them alone. I hope ya understand, Ruth. I surely do miss you. Life just ain't the same without cha."

I tiptoe to bed and cry myself to sleep that night. Momma loved this place.

"I work hard. I milk the cow and cook all the meals. I clean the cabin and wash the clothes in the creek. I bathe Timothy and pick flowers for Momma's grave. My day starts when the sun comes up and it ends late at night. I never complain because we are together as a family and Momma is not far away on the hill. I promised Momma, and Papa always says a person is only as good as their word. I figure that is for kids to. My word is who I am. How can we go away and leave Momma here all alone?"

I close my eyes, as a few tears slide down my cheek. Reaching for the covers, I cover my head. Papa has enough problems with Momma being gone then to worry about me crying and being a baby. I must toughen up and be more of a help to Papa, and take care of the baby.

Having made up my mind, I drift off to sleep, dreaming of picking flowers and singing songs with Momma. The sun is shining and I can hear Momma singing. My whole body relaxes and the troubles of the day disappear like a mist when the sun comes out.

"Momma may be in the grave but a part of her will always be with me."

Chapter Three

Timothy cries a lot. I think he misses Momma. I move Timothy's bed closer to mine. I take him for walks outside and he seems to really enjoy the sunshine and being outdoors. He is starting to see things now and sometimes he even smiles that toothless smile of his, which makes me laugh.

One week after another pass and time seems to stand still. Then a covered wagon pulls around the curve and I hurry into the house to put on a clean dress. I had just finished working with the mules and my dress is dirty. I hurriedly raked a comb through my hair and changed Timothy's cloth. Taking a damp cloth I wipe his face, there is something sticky around his mouth. I can't have strangers think I can't take proper care of my brother; I put a shirt on him that Momma had made last winter out of scraps from Papa's torn shirts. She also made dresses just in case he was a girl.

I turn just in time to see Papa inviting them into the cabin. I feel proud that the cabin is clean and both Timothy and I are presentable.

With a big smile: "Please come in and sit with us for awhile." I motion to the chairs around the table. Momma would have been proud of my manners. I didn't have much use for them way out here, but remember how Momma always said that bad manners would lose you friends faster than lightening.

The man is almost as tall as Papa and has red hair and a beard like Papa. He laughs a lot and Timothy takes a shine to him right away. He says his name is Ralph Higgins and introduces his wife, Maggie. She is heavy-set and real jolly. She comes over to where I am standing and puts her arms around me and gives me a big hug.

"I ain't seen another female in what seems like months. Honey, you're a sight for sore eyes."

"Please, sit and could I get you some cool water from our well. It taste real good." I look from Mr. Higgins and then at her. I give them the biggest smile I can muster up.

"Darling, I would rather you just sit and tell me all about yourself and that fine little brother you have in your arms. The men can bring in the water while they talk outside and leave us women to do our own talking." She puts out her arms for Timothy and I slip him over to her with a smile.

"Now ain't he just the cutest thing ya ever saw, Ralph?" When he didn't answer she turns around and sees that the men have already left the cabin for the water.

"Aw well, what do men know anyway?" She smells him and smiles.

There is nothing as sweet as the smell of a baby." She looks up at me.

"Come and sit down and tell me all about yourself. How old are ya? Do ya like living out here in this valley? What cha think of these beautiful mountains?" Maggie smiles and talks and plays with Timothy all at the same time.

"I am not sure exactly how old I am. I know I have lived six winters though. I love the mountains. They protect us from the strong cold winds in the winter and shade us during the summer as the sunsets. There isn't anything prettier than the sun coming up over that mountain over there. My Momma says that is east. The one behind us is west. The one over there, although it is pretty far away is north and it doesn't block the cold winds, but all the trees slows it down a mite. Momma is buried up on that hill to the south. She is facing east for the rising sun."

"My your educated. I bet you even know how to read and write words."

"Yes, Momma use to teach me. I am not learning any new words anymore. Papa will one day start me back to reading the Bible. Right now, it is too hard for him, losing Momma and all." I feel the sadness threatening to squeeze my heart and make me tear up, so I give a big smile and turn to get the tin cups for the water the men are bringing in, just in time.

"Sara, the Higgins are going to eat supper with us. Once you get them their water, please stir up the fire and I will fetch the meat." He smiles and it is the first time I have seen him smile since Momma went away. My hearts skips a few beats just to see him smile again.

"It is a real pleasure to meet you. Please call me Maggie, I am not a whole lot older than Sara, and I am not use to being called Mrs. Higgins yet. We were married on the wagon train. Ralph and I are moving west. We are going to start us a family when we get there. I want a whole bassel of youngins. The more the better, I say. We are going to have cows and horses and build us a fine cabin with room for everybody." Maggie talks and reminds me of the older girls on the wagon train that were in a hurry to get married and start a family. I am happy that I am in no hurry to leave Papa and Timothy.

I sit down long enough to give Timothy his milk. I am trying to spoon-feed him when Maggie sits down next to me.

"Honey. Can I show you a different way to feed him? It will make it a lot easier on you and he will enjoy it a lot more himself. It won't take as long to fill him up either."

"I am always willing to learn. If it will fill him up faster maybe he will start sleeping all night." I hand him over, but inside I feel uneasy. Maybe I ain't good enough to take care of Timmy if I am already doing it wrong.

"Get me that rag over there and watch us." Maggie takes Timothy and sits him on her lap.

Turning him around where his head is resting on the inside of her elbow, she dips the rag into the cup of milk and sticks it into Timothy's mouth. At first he tries to spit it out but then he taste the milk and starts to suck on the rag. It isn't long before Maggie can't dip the rag fast enough to keep Timothy sucking. He finishes off the cup of milk in no time and his eyelids are getting heavy, as he tries to keep them open.

Maggie gently squeezes his tummy and it is hard. I come over and try and smile. There is very little wasted milk and it didn't take as long to feed him this way. Plus he seemed to really like to suck on the corner of the rag.

"I bet he won't wake before sun up now. How did you know how to do that?" I gently pick up Timmy and cuddle him in my arms, gently rocking him back and forth, by twisting my body.

"When I was little, my Momma had two babies at the same time. We older children took turns feeding them. It just seemed natural to let them suck the milk out of the rag. It sure wasn't as messy as trying to spoon-feed them. Can you imagine all those little hands and arms waving about, Lord all mighty couldn't keep the milk in the spoons." Maggie laughs and I quickly join her.

"Now, lets lay this little guy down and we will get started on cooking that venison. I ain't had good deer meat in a long time. One gets tired of eating dried meat all the time. It will be good to eat tasty and soft food."

After I lay him down, Maggie turns Timothy to lay him on his side and props a rolled baby blanket behind his back.

"Why did you do that? I always just lay him down." I know that Maggie has a lot of things she can teach me and I want to know them all before they move on.

"Well, when you have a little one like this, you lay them on their side after feeding them because they might spit some of their milk back up and if they are on their side, the milk will just run out their mouths. Most of them sleep with their mouths open just a bit. If they are on their backs, the milk goes back down and the babies can choke. I even heard where some babies died from being on their backs.

My dear sweet Momma always insisted we put them on their sides. Then next time we put them on the other side. This way they don't get a flat head. Their little heads are still soft and growing. If they lay all the time on their back or on one side, the head will be flat there. So if a mother wants her babies to have nice round heads, she makes sure they sleep on a different side every time they lay down. Now, when they get big enough to roll over, it won't matter anymore. They will roll over by themselves and have nice round heads, one must also protect the soft spot on top of the head."

"The soft spot? All of him is soft." I don't know of any particular spot that is softer than another part. I have bathed him and never saw or felt one.

"Yes, come of feel right here on top of his head. This will be hard, like yours is now when the bones grow closer together. Sometimes the baby has a hard time being born and God made the head where the bones can move a little bit so the head and body can be born. It is safe to touch it, just be careful not to bump it or hit it."

"I am learning so much while you're here. What if I don't learn it all before you leave?"

"Oh sweet girl, if I stayed and we both lived until we are old, we won't be able to learn it all. My momma taught me that when I am too old to learn anymore, then I am dieing." Maggie takes me in her arms and gives me a gentle hug.

"I guess your right about that. My momma use to say your never too old to learn all the time." The hug feels so good; I really need some affection right now. I miss Momma's hugs and constant teaching me, she was very patient with me.

"Now that we have this little guy falling asleep, lets get started on cleaning up so we can cook supper for those men."

I look around and wonder what she means by cleaning up. The cabin has been swept and the beds are made. I look around and frown, then look back at Maggie.

Maggie is stacking the dishes as if she is going to wash them. She puts on an apron and turns and asks me where the well is.

"We will get the fire hot for the water and then wash the dishes, that way we will have them clean for supper. While the dishes are being washed we will add more wood to the fire to make sure it is good and hot for cooking. By the time the men get back we will have the cabin clean and a fine meal cooked. It won't be hard because we will be working together and talking. That always makes time pass by faster." Maggie smiles and picks up the bucket to go and get fresh water for cleaning.

When she returns, she puts the water on the fire to get it hot. Then she turns and starts putting away the dishes that are already clean. She finds places under the sink on the shelves. When everything clean had been put away and out of sight, she drew the hand-sewed curtains together to hide what is under the sink. Folding the dishcloth she turns and looks around, and sees me watching her. I guess she realizes I am kind of hurt by the look in my eyes cause she immediately comes over to me.

"Sara, when I was your age I didn't know about how to go about making a house look like a home. I was more interested in finding toads and lizards then washing dishes or hanging up clothes on the line to dry. Then we moved to the city and I was invited over to my friend's homes and they lived in some fine houses. Everything was put away and the houses would almost sparkle from being so clean. At first I was afraid to touch anything, scared I would get it dirty. When I got home, I looked around my own house and I could see ways to make my house look better and cleaner. I started cleaning and my Momma was so surprised. She seemed to always be either about to have a baby or having one in her arms. She was tired but she tried to make our house a home. When I started doing the cleaning, it got easier to keep it up then to wait until it got dirty. We started having more people come to visit us, and I felt pride in our home. It wasn't nothing fancy like the other houses but it was clean and it was ours. I felt so much better and my folks seemed to be happier too. Now I do it without thinking about it."

I back away and look around the house.

"Well, I guess it could use some work. My Momma spent the last week or so in bed before the Timothy came and I spent my time watching Papa pull up stumps or fetching the water and doing some laundry for Momma."

"If you like, I can teach ya what I learned. It will give ya something to do while Timothy is sleeping. Ya can't leave the house anyway." Maggie grins when she sees my smiling face. We are friends again and no hurt feelings.

Maggie takes the dishwater and then throws it on the floor. I jump up on the hearth when she does that.

"What cha go and do that for?" I can't believe what I just saw.

"To mop the floor. These wood floors like to hang onto dust and dirt. With everyone walking in and out they bring in dirt from the outside. One day Timothy will be crawling around on these floors. Now think about it; your Pa walks around those mules all day long and he steps in their droppings and in the dirt and mud and then he tracks that back into the house where Timothy will be crawling through. Do you really want him crawling through mule manure?" She waves her hand across the floor when she talks.

"NO. He puts his fingers in his mouth. Your right, I will be mopping these floors everyday."

I hop down and move the benches away from the table so she can mop under the table. As Maggie mops, I go in front of her moving boxes and Papa's chair out of the way. Soon all the mop water is swept out the front door and the last of the water is thrown on the porch and it is also swept off, leaving those boards fresh washed.

"There, that done, lets get to cooking. I will need your help here, too."

Maggie has me go about gathering the ingredients and she puts them in a big bowl. She lets me mix up the ingredients because I said I was having trouble baking bread like Momma. She stands next to me, making sure I do it right, and telling me little hints that I might not know. When it is done, she covers the bowl with a wet cloth and sets it in the window.

"Why did you do that? I remember seeing Momma doing it but I never asked. Why don't we just bake it?" I want to understand why things are done the way they are.

"It will make the dough rise. Then the bread will be light and fluffy."

Maggie immediately starts washing the dishes we just used. I realize I wait until after supper, at the end of the day, to wash dishes for the whole day.

When the dough is big and fluffy, I get to beat it down and then cover it so to let it rise again. I am really enjoying my cooking lessons and time with Maggie. I have a deep longing learn to do things right; always have so Momma use to tell me.

"Next we clean out the fireplace." Maggie doesn't even take time to rest a mite.

I gather up the bucket and the scoop Papa sets beside the hearth and begin to shovel the soot and ashes into the bucket.

"I know there is a good reason, but I don't know what it is." I laugh as I scoop the ashes, watching my hands turn black from the soot.

"The ashes will keep the air from making a real hot fire. We need a hot fire by which to cook. By keeping the ashes cleaned out, air will get to the logs and flames." Maggie's voice is strong and she never makes me feel my questions are dumb.

"I wish you could stay forever. Settle here and not go on further. How old are you?"

"I would love nothing better but my husband has his heart set on Texas and I am fourteen. We were married just before my birthday."

I follow her outside to the well where she dumps the ashes and scatters them all around.

"Always, put your ashes here. Then next spring have your father plow the ashes under the ground and plant your garden. The ashes will help your plants be strong and fruitful and the water in the well will be close by so you won't have to carry it very far." Maggie stands up and rubs her back, the way Momma use to when she was with Timothy.

"We will not be here come spring. I think Papa is going to take us back east because we are too much trouble." I feel tears sting my eyes and know I am going to cry. Before the tears could leave my eyes, Maggie has me in her arms and hugs me.

"That will be a shame, but, this is dangerous land. I know he is doing this out of love, not from you being too much trouble. He wants to protect you. There are many dangers out here and the city offers more for the children. There are schools and churches and people there who can help take care of you. He is doing this out of love. I can see in his eyes how much he loves you. They are so full of love. You are his life." She smoothes my hair, and brushes the tears away with her handkerchief from her pocket.

"I try not to be too much trouble. I help all I can and take care of Timothy, but he cries and I don't know what to do. I think he misses Momma. The cow is going dry and she doesn't give us enough milk anymore. I try to feed Timothy other food but he spits it back out. I think all he wants is milk."

"We just came from the market. We wanted to buy a cow but they were sold out so we bought a fresh nanny goat. She has a kid with her but she is old enough to be weaned. Lets go see if Timothy likes goat's milk. If he does, maybe, we can work something out."

When we caught the goat, Maggie gets down and shows me how to milk her. It wasn't that much different than milking the cow, only lower to the ground and a much smaller bag.

We brought the milk in and I watch as Maggie strains it through a clean flour-sack cloth.

"Why did you do that? I just pour it into the wells bucket for safe keeping." There is just so much to learn and a reason for everything. I wonder if I will learn enough before they move on?

"To get any trash out. Sometimes the wind can blow in dust or leaves or even twigs. Sometimes the goat or cow can stomp the dirt and get it in the milk, or a fly could fall in it. This is just a way to keep the milk pure for drinking."

We dip a corner of the sack in the milk and let Timothy suck on it.

At first he doesn't like the taste. It doesn't taste anything like cows milk. Then, he starts sucking and I can't feed him fast enough. He really likes the milk and he likes sucking the cloth.

Maggie says it is important for them to suck to live. This is how they learn to swallow.

When the men come back in Timothy is sound asleep with a belly full of goat's milk and a clean cloth. I anxiously tell Papa the story and he makes a deal to trade some dried deer meat for the goat.

Meanwhile, I pray that now Papa will let us stay with him in this valley.

That afternoon Maggie starts teaching me how to mend Papa's shirts.

"I saw Momma do this but I was always too busy trying to see what Papa was doing. His chores seemed more fun than sitting around an old cabin sewing. If I had only known, maybe, I would have paid more attention."

"Some things are not for us to know. If you had known, you would have been very sad and maybe afraid. That would have made it harder for you and your mother. This way she went in peace, knowing you are brave and strong and very smart and will learn all you need to know. She must have been very proud of you."

"We were very close. She taught me a lot of things and so does Papa. I learn fast. I am just not big enough to do all the things she used to do. I wish she didn't have to leave us. I am not questioning God, understand, just I surely miss her a powerful lot."

"Yes, I am sure you do. Now, lets see how you're seam is coming. Yes, you are doing fine." Fingering the material, she checks the shirt seam and pulls the material tight to make sure the seams holds.

"It don't look very straight or fancy but it holds. I think maybe now I can start on making the seams more even and straighter." I am laughing but deep down I feel really proud. I am learning how to sew and one day maybe I can make Timothy some clothes or Papa a shirt.

Our bread turns out perfect. With fresh goats milk to drink, the bread would taste even better. I knew Momma had sent these fine people to keep from Papa taking us away.

When Papa comes in, he is surprised to see flowers on the table, and the table all set, with fresh bread, deer meat, and beans and gravy. There are no dirty dishes on the cabinets and the floors have been mopped. Even Timothy has on clean clothes after his bath. He didn't say anything, but the look on his face spoke more than any words he would have said.

The next morning, after eating biscuits and gravy, and cleaning the kitchen, putting everything away, the Higgins leave. I am sad to see them go, however, I am sure now that I can take care of Papa and Timothy. They said if we ever come to Texas to stop and see them and they will repay our kindness. I owe Maggie and one day I hope to repay her with a visit.

The nanny goat calls for her baby for a few days than stops. Timothy also stops crying as much with the goat's milk. Seems it is better for his tummy than the cow's milk anyway.

Every day Timothy and I go out and pick flowers for Momma's grave. We stake the goat in a different place every day so she will have lots of grass and weeds to eat. This way she will give lots of milk to drink and cook with. My cooking gets better and I am keeping the cabin like a woman would keep it. It makes me feel proud when I look around the cabin, looking for something out of place or something that needs to be done and can't find anything. Even my mending improves and Papa never wears a shirt that needs mending any more.

Timothy loves the outdoors and always coos at the sights. I made a sling where I can carry him on my back and still pick flowers or carry noon meal to Papa. This frees up my hands for food and cool water for him to drink.

I always put Timothy under the old oak tree that has become our special tree. There is only one place a person can crawl under but once inside, the shade is cool because the sun can't get thru. There are hardly any weeds or undergrowth so I don't have to worry about Timothy putting them in his mouth. Even the smallest plants cannot live without the sunlight. There is just enough sunlight to cause the shadows to move when the breeze blows. The shadows will gently dance back and forth. The dance puts Timothy to sleep every time.

The center of the tree is actually five trees that grew together as one. Only they split and circle, meeting at their trunks higher up. I climb in this cavity with Timothy and hide. Then I call for Papa. He pretends that he doesn't know where we are and comes looking for us. He walks around and around the tree, trying to peer in. I hold Timothy real close to me, against my chest, and tell him to be real quiet. He enjoys the game so much he really tries to be quiet.

When Papa comes closer, he calls and calls and then he jumps down on his knees and yells BOO and we scream. Then he comes in and wrestles us to the ground and tickles us.

Timothy loves this and laughs very loud and so do I. Even Papa seems happier these days. He never mentions going back east anymore.

Papa saved this tree just for us. I asked him not to cut it down. It is our special tree. Like the one on the hill was Momma's and my special tree. This is where Timothy said his first word. He said tree, well it is more ree but we knew what he means. He points to it when we are at the cabin and keeps saying ree ree ree. This means he is ready to go to the tree and see Papa.

I spread a blanket and lay Timothy on the blanket and then put the food out. Sometimes, I have to go ahead and give Timothy something to eat; he is starting to nibble on real food now. I don't think he swallows it yet, just chews on it.

After we eat, Papa takes one last drink of cool water and crawls out from under the tree, then goes back to work. The sweat has dried from his shirt and he always says he can work until dark because of the fine meal we brought him. I know he can work because he doesn't have any choice. We have to survive this winter.

I pack everything back up while I wait for Timothy to wake up and then we take everything back to the cabin.

I start supper and milk the goat and clean what still needs cleaning, then, I mend another shirt. I have even started sewing Timothy a shirt out of an old dress of mine. It was too small for me now and I can use the material for Timothy.

After supper, I stand at the window and watch Papa. Every evening he goes out and sits on the stump and looks up at the stars. Sometimes I can hear him talking to Momma. This is when I turn and leave them to their private time.

Papa starts to work with me in the evenings on the Bible lessons again. I haven't been reading or doing my numbers and he wants to get me started back on them least I forget. I really don't mind because I enjoy reading and writing. He also starts me on drawing pictures. He says back east there are places where people pay money to come and see drawings and paintings that hang on a wall.

When he first tells me this I laugh. I cannot picture in my mind people paying hard earned money just to see a picture someone drew. Papa says some pictures are so real like, one would expect the people to speak to them or walk away. He says some are of funny pictures and it makes people laugh. If a picture can make someone happy, then they would pay money to see it and even a lot more money to buy it.

I can't even imagine this. I remember coming out on the wagon train and some people did not have enough money to buy flour or salt or coffee and sugar. Momma said we needed to share with these people because God takes care of those who share what he gives them, so we did. It never hurt us none because we always had plenty. It also made Momma happy to share. Papa would help the men work on their wagons and help dig them out when they got stuck in the mud. They set good examples to follow. I think that is more important than reading about it in books.

One bright sunny day when Timothy is sleeping next to me, up on the hill under the tree, I look up from my reading and I see a wagon come around the bend in the road that leads to our cabin. I wave to Papa in the field, pointing to the bend, he looks and takes off his hat and wipes the sweat off his forehead with his right forearm, then replaces his hat and starts to walk toward the cabin where the wagon is heading. He leaves the mules tied to the plow in the field, for now.

I pick up Timmy and start down the hill, watching him to see what he does. If he slaps his hip with his hat, we are suppose to go hide under the tree, but he doesn't seem worried. I walk slowly and watch the covered wagon come around the last turn and the people wave at Papa.

So it is someone we know, by the way Papa waves back. They are still too far away from me to see who they are, but I shade my eyes and strain to see anyway. They seem excited to see Papa. They slow down and the mules barely walk forward. I see a blond boy stick his head out of the back of the wagon. Who is it?

The wagon pulls up and stops and the man jumps down and gives Papa a bear hug. Papa is slapping him on the back. Yes, it is someone we know, all right, and I pick up my pace.

The boy jumps out of the back and comes around to where the men are. Papa points my direction and the boy starts running up the hill towards me.

I have Timothy on my hip and when I recognize Johnny Holbrook from the wagon train. We were best friends on the train all the way out here. They stopped and settled about fifty miles back and now they are in our front yard. I am so excited. Not only is he the first kid I have seen since we left the wagon train but he is my best friend.

I pick up pace and almost fall, Timothy is throwing me off balance. I want to run but I am afraid of hurting my brother, so I walk as fast as I dare going down hill.

When we finally meet, I see Johnny's excited face and he is talking and I am talking and neither one of us knows what the other one is saying. I ask questions and he is asking questions and when I try to answer his question he is answering mine. Soon we are both laughing.

Mrs. Holbrook comes over and takes Timothy from my arms and hugs him. I see the sadness in her face and I know that Papa has told her about Momma. Timothy loves for people to fuss over him so he doesn't mind.

I invite them into the cabin, thanking God and Maggie that the cabin is clean and has fresh flowers on the table and no dirty dishes.

I get out the tin cups for fresh cool water and go out to the well, but Johnny lowers the bucket for me and pulls the rope through the pulley when the bucket is full. Then I have him raise the milk and meat bucket. I take in some fresh goats milk in case someone would rather have that instead of water. The whole time Johnny is talking and laughing. He has all sorts of tales to tell me.

When we get back in, Mrs. Holbrook is still playing with Timothy and the men are sitting at the table talking. I pour the water and ask if any would like cool goats milk and Mr. Holbrook said he would love some, he hadn't had any in a long time.

Mrs. Holbrook tells me for us youngins to go outside and play, to enjoy ourselves. We didn't need to be told twice. Before she could get the words out of her mouth we are out the door.

"Want to go to the creek?" I am hot and wading in the creek sounds like a good way to cool off.

"Sure. I am plum tuckered out from riding in the back of that wagon. I thought when we stopped that we wouldn't be going nowhere for a spell. My Pa says that there is free land in Texas and he wants to get there and homestead us a ranch before it is all gone. He says I can have my own horse."

"Wow, your own horse? That sounds good. Might be worth moving for that."

"Yeah, maybe. Shoot, maybe I can break it to ride by myself. I ain't afraid of getting bucked off or nothing."

"That sounds dangerous. Horses can kick and stomp you into the ground. Might be better to let a man do it first and then you just have to ride it and teach it to lead."

"Why, I am pretty near being a man. The way I figure it, because I am smaller, the horse will have a harder time getting me off. Those big fellow's get off balance and fall too far one direction or the other and off they go. Maybe I will even get me a baby horse and start training it from the beginning who is boss. We can become friends and he won't be afraid of me or nuthin and trust that I ain't going to hurt em."

"Lets sit down on this rock and take our shoes off and we can stick our feet in the cool water." Johnny points to a boulder that stretches out over the shadow creek.

I sit down and take off my shoes that are getting too small for me and my toes are already starting to hurt.

Johnny sits down next to me. Taking off his new boots as he tells me about where they lived.

"There were other kids there but not like you. The girls were afraid of getting dirty or their hair messed up and the boys were sissies too. They liked to play stickball but were afraid to catch the ball if it was hit hard because it would hurt their poor little hands. A bunch of babies if ya ask me."

"At least you had kids to play with. Other then my baby brother, there hasn't been any kids to play with. I don't think there are any kids on these mountains or in the valleys. Never heard of none."

"I saw ya carrying em. Where's yer Mom. I didn't see her."

"She died right after my brother was born. She had to go. She tried real hard to stay here but she couldn't. She is buried up there on that hill that we were walking down. We went up there to put flowers on her grave." I nod towards the hill.

"Gosh darn it. I opened my mouth and now you're all sad. I didn't know."

"No, it is not your fault. I am all right. I have gotten use to her not being around no more. I miss her but I stay busy with taking care of Papa and Timothy."

Without warning. Johnny jumps in the creek and splashes me.

I scream as the cold water hits me and jump in after him. The two of us kick the cold water on each other and run in circles like two young pups. Screaming and hollering at each other and the time that we have been separated is lost and all that matters is this moment.

This is the first time I have stepped back and become a kid again. My face feels bright and the laughter is something I believed I would never do again after Maggie left. It is not long before both of us are soaking wet and our laughter is dieing down. We go back to the rock and sit on it to warm up under the sun and dry off before going back to the cabin.

"So you been taking care of the baby by yourself?" Johnny searches for something to say.

"Yeah. Papa works the fields and I take care of the cabin and the cooking and Timothy."

"I would say your pretty near being a wife without having no husband."

Laughing; "I do all the things my mother did, even sewing now."

"Why don't cha talk to your Papa and get him to come to Texas with us. That way we know we will have someone to play along the way and then when we get there my ma can help with your brother."

"I don't think Papa will leave Momma. He thought about going back east a while back but has changed his mind. I really don't think he will leave her."

"We could dig her up and take her with us."

"JOHNNY!!! We couldn't dig her up! That wouldn't be right."

"We dig up the box and take it. No one will have to know she is in the box."

"She is not in a box. She is wrapped in a quilt. We didn't have a box to put her in." My voice cracks and Johnny realizes he spoke too soon.

"We could get a box. That is if your Pa really wants to come with us. Won't hurt nothing to ask."

"Telling ya, he won't leave. Come on, we better be getting back. I had fun Johnny. Thank Ya." I didn't feel like playing anymore.

"Look, can ya see the gold in the water? It's real gold. It will bring a good price back in town, we could gather it up and be rich. Your Pa won't have to work no more. Heck, maybe my folks will forget about

Texas if we can get rich here. Come on, lets get that gold." Johnny jumps back into the water and I follow. His excitement is catching.

We gather up the shining gold stones and store them on the boulder we were just sitting on. We laugh and with each trip back to the boulder we come up with something new we are going to buy with our money. The more we gather; the bigger our dreams become. We are talking faster with each handful.

"I know, lift up your skirt." Johnny has his arms full of small stones.

"YOU WANT ME TO DO WHAT? JOHNNY HOLBROOK!" I drop what rocks I have back into the water and put my hands on my hips. My face burns red with anger and my eyes squint into small slits.

"Just to put the rocks in. We can haul more, faster if we use your skirt to carry them. I will pack your skirt and you empty them on the rock while I gather up more. We will work as a team. What did you think I meant?"

"Never you mind. Just keep your mind on those rocks." I lift up my skirt to just above my knees, and Johnny starts putting the shinny gold stones on the material.

The water from the rocks is running down my legs and tingling me. I laugh and encourage Johnny to put more stones in, that I can carry them.

"Your no sissy, that's for sure." Johnny drops more stones in and bends over to recover the ones he dropped back into the water.

"How much do ya think we will get from all this gold?"

"Enough to buy the whole state if we want to. Look, we haven't even started getting all the rocks just here in the creek. I will have to talk my folks into helping us find the place where they come from. Then your Pa and my Pa will have to start the mining of the gold. They will be so busy digging; it will have to be up to us to haul all the gold back into town to collect our money. Why we could fill up the covered wagon and haul enough gold in to buy the whole mountain in our first haul."

"Won't that make the wagon too heavy to pull?" I feel the excitement and begin to share the dream with Johnny.

"Heck, we will have to use your mules with our mules. With the four of them, surely they can pull the wagon back to town. Think about it, those mules pulled the wagons from New York to Virginia, over those mountain passes and in the snow and mud. Carrying just these small rocks won't be that hard."

I walk slowly over to the boulder, being careful where I step so as not to fall on the slippery rocks. My heart beats faster then it would if I was running. In my mind I can see Johnny and his family staying around and carrying these rocks is going to make it happen. I would rather have them around then all the riches in the world. We would not be alone anymore.

Mrs. Holbrook calls for us to come and eat. Johnny yells back we will be right there. He turns and puts one more handful of rocks in my skirt and holds onto my shoulders to balance me as I carry the heaviest load yet.

Sitting on the rocks, we talk about all our plans and things we are going to buy with our gold.

Johnny gets his boots on faster then I can get mine on. He stands and offers me a hand up and I take it and he pulls me up.

"How we going to get all these rocks back to the cabin to show our parents?" I look at the large pile of rocks.

"We will just take a few and leave the rest for now. Our Pa's can come and get them with the buckboard. Won't they be surprised!!"

I steady myself beside him and smile. "I guess your right about that."

All of a sudden Johnny leans over and kisses me on the cheek, takes off running before I can sock him; then turns and yells back.

"Last one to the cabin is a rotten egg." He keeps running toward the cabin.

I put my hand to my cheek. "You kissed me!!" I yell at his back. He keeps right on going without slowing down, laughing.

I look back at the water and try to decide if I should go back and wash it off or if I should keep it.

As my hand gently touches the cheek, I slowly smile a little smile and then decide I am going to keep it, forever. Smiling I walk back to the cabin, taking my time, enjoying the intense smell of the spring flowers and all the birds singing. It is like everything witnessed the kiss and it made them all very happy, they couldn't help but share their happiness with everything around them. It didn't compare though with what I am feeling deep inside though. I am not sure if my feet are touching the ground. My stomach is full of butterflies and my heart is racing. I want this moment to last forever.

The Holbrook's are stepping out on the porch, as we come around the wagon.

"I was just getting ready to call you again to come in to eat. I have supper all ready." Mrs. Holbrook smiles when she sees how wet we are. She knew we had a great time playing.

"Looks like you two didn't waste any time in getting back to your old ways." Mr. Holbrook looks at us and smiles then adds:

"Johnny really needs to be with someone he likes to be around, he is very picky on who he chooses for friends."

Both of us start at the same time about our great find. Mrs. Holbrook wants us to dry off so we can eat but we won't be still long enough for her to dry our hair. I am talking to my Pa and Johnny words are running together that no one can make sense out of what it is that has us so excited.

Finally, Mr. Holbrook raises his hand up and has everyone stop talking. Then taking a hold of Johnny's shoulders he asks; "What is going on? What has the two of you spouting off like a couple of chickens with a fox in the hen house?"

Both of us start talking again, this time faster then before.

Mr. Holbrook starts laughing.

"One at a time. Lets start with Sara. She seems calmer. Sara, tell us what is going on." He takes one hand off Johnny's shoulder and puts his finger over his lips to let Johnny know to remain quiet. He obeyed but not happy about it.

"Well; Johnny and I found GOLD. Lots of gold, we gathered up a whole bunch from the creek and we need the buckboard to bring it back to the cabin."

"Yea, Pa. We are going to be rich. There is enough gold to buy these mountains and we will need your help to get it loaded and taken to town." Johnny couldn't stay quiet.

"Gold, huh?" Smiling the two men grin at each other.

"How about you showing us where this gold is." Papa steps up and puts his arm around me.

"Wait just a darn minute. What about supper? It is hot and ready to eat." Mrs. Holbrook stands on the porch with her hands on her hips, her words sound firm but her eyes are sparkling and she knows supper will have to wait.

We walk back to the creek with our fathers. We never stop talking about all our plans and how we are going to be the richest people in the valley, maybe the whole wide world.

One look at the pile of stones on the boulder and the men look at each other, with a knowing expression. We see this change of looks and both of us turn to each other with questioning looks. Why aren't they excited like us?

"Well, don't cha see the gold? Why ain't cha excited? I know there will be a lot of work but Sara and I are going to cut you in. We will rich. There is enough for all of us. Why ain't cha excited?" Johnny is looking from one father to the other.

"This is not going to be what ya'll want to hear. Now there have been some grown men that were fooled by these stones."

"Fooled? What cha mean fooled? Don't cha see it is gold?" Johnny doesn't like the way the men are acting, not one bit.

"This is what they call Fools Gold. It is not the real gold. A lot of people have been fooled by these stones, your not the first and won't be the last. I see the two of you have worked very hard. We are sorry but they just aren't worth anything. They are just pretty rocks. I am sorry, kids."

He puts his arm around Johnny's shoulder and Papa picks me up and we return to the cabin. No one says a word. The men know the disappointment we feel. There just weren't no words to make us feel better.

Once prayer is said, supper is eaten in complete silence. No one knows what to say to ease the disappointment we feel. The words just didn't seem to come or are good enough to ease our pain. Neither one of us feel much like eating.

After supper and the dishes are done, the men go to the barn to tend to the animals and Mrs. Holbrook walks out onto the porch where we are sitting on the steps, being very quiet.

Sitting down between us, she puts her arms around us.

"I remember when I was young, before I met your Pa or your folks, I had dreams of living in a big white house on a hill. I would have a red horse with a white blaze and four white socks to ride. Everyone in town would look at me and think how pretty I was and how much they wished they could be like me. Then as I grew older I realized I didn't want people to look at me and wish they could be like me. It is best they are themselves and that everyone be different. I don't need a big house on a hill; I need my family to be around me instead. I never got the horse but I got a good man and a wonderful son that makes me happier than all the big white houses and the fancy horses could ever make me. As I grew older, I discovered these people with all those fancy things live in fear that someone will one day take that away from them.

How very sad for them. They will never know the joy that comes from having dreams that may never come true but at least they are able to dream. They will never know the love of a friendship because they are too afraid to open their hearts to be a friend to others. They live lonely lives and when they are old they have no stories to tell their children.

You have something more valuable then all the gold in the world. You have a very strong friendship and stories to tell your children from the wagon train and the things you did together and someday, in the future, this story will be a funny story to share with your children. The day two very good friends discovered dreams of riches together and made big plans only to have them crushed by stones of yellow. One thing that makes a friendship last a lifetime is sharing not just the good times also the hard times together. Your friendship is more valuable than all the gold in the world.

Ask yourselves this one question; would you want that gold if you thought it would destroy your friendship? That is what happens sometimes when money comes between friends. They become enemies."

"We will never be enemies, will we Sara?"

"No. We are friends for life. I would rather have both but if I can't, then I don't want the gold." I hang my head but look sideways at Johnny questionly.

"I really wanted that to be real gold, Momma. Sara and I made plans together. If I had to choose between our friendship and the gold though, I would choose Sara too."

"That is what I thought. You two have something more valuable than money can buy. Cherish this time and remember this story to tell your children." She gets up and walks back into the cabin.

"Now, we are back to where we were before we went to the creek."

"Not really. We had fun, cooled off, and now we have a story to tell." I smile at Johnny and then laugh. Johnny soon joins me in my laughter.

"Boy do we ever have a great story to tell. I can also tell the one about the first girl I ever kissed." He jumps up and runs out under the stars so I will not see his red face.

I just sit there and watch. I didn't know what to say. I just understand this also means they will be going away again.

I play in the dirt with my toes trying to take my mind off what will happen in the morning.

Johnny comes back and sits close. "What is wrong? You look sad."

"Just thinking. This means that you will be leaving tomorrow. Texas is a lot further away and this time we won't be seeing each other again. We can't pretend we will."

"I am going to talk to my Pa. Maybe he will talk your Pa into coming with us."

"We already had this talk, he won't leave Momma. That is just the way it is."

The men come back around the cabin and see the kids sitting close on the steps.

Their faces look like someone had just killed a dog.

"Pa, can the Andersons come with us on the wagon train to Texas?"

"I think that can be arranged if they want to come. There is plenty of room in Texas from what we hear. Lots of free land."

"I thank you for the invite, maybe someday. Timothy is too small to take on the trip and I have settled here for now." He glances up the hill and looks back; "The timing is wrong right now."

Mrs. Holbrook starts to offer to help with the baby but when she sees him looking up at the grave she decides it is too soon to expect him to pack up his family and move.

"Come on in. I am looking forward to you men singing tonight and entertaining us."

Chapter Four

The next morning, after a hearty breakfast, the Holbrook's get ready to leave for Texas.

Papa and Mr. Holbrook are hitching up their mules and Mrs. Holbrook insists on cleaning the kitchen and we go outside to play.

"I wish your Papa would change his mind and ya come with us. It won't be the same without you on the wagon train. I know there will be other kids and all, but I would rather you be there."

"I would like to go, too. My place is with Papa and Timothy and if Papa says no then that is what he means and we stay here. I know him pretty good and he does not change his mind very often. Momma use to be able to talk to him, and get him to change his mind, sometimes, she was the only one who could talk some sense into him. I have never seen anyone else be able to talk him into doing something he had set his mind against.

Momma use to say he was born with a stubborn streak a mile wide. I think she was right." I hang my head, folding my hands in my lap.

"Sure is going to be lonely on that trip without you to play with."

"There will be other boys and girls and you will make new friends. I bet by the time you get to Texas you won't even remember me. You go and raise your horses and maybe someday we will come that way and visit you. This is not good-bye but just so long, until we meet again. You will see. We will meet again."

"I believe you. When we left the wagon train to get that farm, I didn't want to say good-bye and you said we would meet again and sure enough we did. I think maybe you know the future, and I believe you. So I am not going to say goodbye, just say until we meet again."

"That's right. Until we meet again." I try hard to fight back the tears.

"Now don't go and cry or anything. It will just make me think you don't believe it."

"I ain't going to cry. I don't cry no more. I am too big to be a baby. I said it so it is true."

The next morning Johnny climbs into the back of the wagon and sits down. Mr. Holbrook, at the front of the wagon, helps his wife up, and then he turns and shakes hands with Papa. I couldn't hear their words, but knew they are serious words by the look on Mr. Holbrook's face.

I stand waving goodbye as the wagon is slowly turned around and they head back up the lane. Papa puts his hand on my shoulder and I look down at it. His hand covers my whole shoulder and his fingers seem to stretch way down. I have never seen another man with such large hands. Everything is large with Papa, including his heart. I look up and see the moisture in his eyes and wonder if he is having second thoughts.

"Sara, what do you say about us getting Sally and you and Timothy riding her and I will ride Clyde and we can go and set more traps. Do you think you can ride and hold onto Timothy, too?"

"Sure I can. Timothy will sit in front of me and I will keep both arms around him and hold onto the reins at the same time. You know how Molly likes to poke around when she has me on her back. She will be even more pokey with Timothy up there too."

I have the biggest smile. I have been looking forward to going with Papa for a long time, and now that Timothy is older, it will be an adventure. I am already planning on what food to pack for the picnic we will have under some tree up in the mountain somewhere.

Once in the cabin, I tell Timothy about our upcoming adventure. Papa is out getting the mules ready and tying on the traps to Clyde's pack. This will not only help provide food for the winter but the furs will make good rugs for the floors, to help keep the cold out and keep the heat in. If he is lucky he will have enough for the windows also. He can't afford for us to get sick. There isn't a doctor around for miles. The nearest town is almost twenty miles away and the doctor has a large territory to cover.

Picking me up, he puts me on Molly's back, while holding Timothy is his other arm.

Setting Timothy in front of me, I immediately wrap my arm around him and he puts Molly's reins in my free hand. Putting his hand on my leg, he looks up at me with a big smile.

"Ya ready?"

"Yes, Oh, NO. I forgot. I packed up a picnic and it is on the table in the cabin."

"Well, I will fetch it and then we can go. I think that was very wise of you to think about bringing food. We can stay out longer and set more traps, now. Your becoming a very smart young lady." He walks around the mule, with his hand on the mules behind, and I beam with pride. I look up at the sky and smile.

"Did ye hear Papa, Momma? He thinks I am wise. We are doing all right."

"Who ye talking to child?" Papa ties the picnic to Clyde.

"Oh, just Momma."

He smiles and starts walking up the hill, leading Clyde and his heavy load behind him.

Molly walks behind Clyde, making sure of her steps; as though she understands her cargo is more precious than anything she has ever carried before.

The trail up the mountain is rocky and sometimes we had to get off the mule so she could climb up the steep parts without us falling off. I walk beside Papa and he carries Timothy. I talk the whole time and Papa laughs at my stories. My imagination is good and I tell him of my plans when I grow up and things I want to do to the cabin before winter.

He listens; the distraction is making the uphill incline easier to climb with my jabbering.

Ever so often, he would stop and set a trap, brushing leaves across the trap with a stick.

Then he would mark the area with a mark on the tree nearest it and an arrow pointing to the trap. This he did with his knife, which he wears on his belt.

When he finds tracks, he points them out to me. I am now walking beside him with Timothy in a sling on my back. Papa came up with this idea, and using old shirts, he instructed me how to make it. I spent several days' hand sewing it and double stitching it to be sure it would hold Timothy's weight. When I finished, I had Papa put Timothy in it and help me get it on.

It fits perfect and we are both proud of the sling and Timothy loves riding in it. Now he can sleep and go wherever I go at the same time. Everyone is happy. It is much easier to carry him then the one I made with him in front of me.

Papa sees where a bear has been scratching a tree and points this out to me.

"The bear stretches his paws up high to not only sharpen the claws but to show the other bears how big and strong he is. This is one of his ways of marking his territory."

"What are the other ways, Papa?" I love lessons about the real world. It makes me want to learn more. There is so much to learn and its not hard like the Bible learning I do.

"He wets on the tree and also does his droppings in other places. The other bears smell these and will go to another area. A female bear may be wanting a mate and she will stay in the area in hopes he will come by and think she is beautiful and is looking for a wife.

Now if she is not interested, she will leave the area to go to another area to look for food or a mate. When a female is looking for a mate she can be dangerous, but when she has a cub or two she is even more dangerous than the male. One must look at the tracks and look around to see if there are smaller tracks around. We don't kill the females unless they are a threat to us. This way, she can produce more bears and we will always have bear meat to eat and furs to keep us warm."

"So we only kill the Papa bears?"

"That's right. They can be very dangerous and they are larger and have more meat. The bear fat is good for greasing a sore or wound and helping to make it well."

"What does the babies do without their Papa?" My voice begins to break.

"The Papa bears don't stay around to be with the cubs. The mother bear would kill him. The Papa bears will kill the cubs and the mother knows this. So as soon as she knows she is going to have babies, she leaves and finds a cave and sleeps all winter. The cubs are born in the winter and they feed off her all winter and when she wakes up, she has one or two babies that are bonded with each other and they know her smell and they are now strong enough to go with her when she goes fishing in the rivers or springs. Maybe we will see some in the river further up. We must keep our distance. There is nothing more dangerous than a mother who thinks their young is in danger. If she smells us, she will come looking for us or run away. Ye can never count on her running away though."

"I would protect Timothy with my life. I think I can understand the Momma Bears."

"I will protect both of you with my life. I might be big as a bear but I love my children and I will take care of you."

"What if the Momma bears dies like Momma?"

"Then the cubs are on their own. Sometimes they get into trouble and don't live very long. Most of the time, they watch other bears from a distance and when the time is right they fish like they saw them do and they eat berries and small animals that they can catch. The first time, is usually, from them playing with the small animals and biting into them. Once they taste blood, they understand these small animals are for eating."

"I think it is better to be human and know who my Papa is and know he will take care of us."

"I think it is better, too. Just think what a lonely life the papa bears live."

"So it is kind to kill the papa bears and put them out of their misery?"

Smiling; "One might think of it like that, I guess."

Maybe now I will not be upset if he kills a bear in front of me. I will not see them as pets or almost human.

We spent the night high on the mountain. While Papa unloads the mules, I hunt near by for firewood. I understand why we did not camp near the stream. When we were above the stream and looked down, two big black bears were fishing and they did not look like they would want to share the area with a man and two children, without eating them, of course.

Sitting around the campfire, Papa tells stories about his childhood in the old country. I am rolling over with laughter at the thought of some of the stunts Papa pulled on his father. Timothy exhausted from the ride and excitement is sound asleep in a quilt, lying next to me.

I thought about telling Papa about Johnny kissing me but decided against it. This is a secret I want to keep. I don't want to explain how I felt about it, because I really don't know how I should have felt, just know I didn't wash that cheek for a week, and only then because Papa commented that I missed my cheek when I took my bath.

The next morning, I help Papa carry traps to different spots. He sets the traps and then would mark the spot and move on. Timothy, just learning to make sounds, talks to himself the whole time he is awake now. Papa gives him a rock to play with and he is talking to the rock. Papa and I laugh and wonder what he thinks he is saying.

Papa points to a buck's tracks.

"This is a big deer. Lets look for a tree where he is sharpening his antlers and that will tell us how big." Papa and I walk around looking at the different trees. I see where a bear has sharpened its claws and chills run up and down my spine. I walk over to the tree and stretch and even standing on my tiptoes I cannot reach half way up the tree mark. This is not a bear I want to meet. I run back to Papa where I feel safe.

Papa points out a tree and we walk softly so as to not disturb the tracks and find this is the tree the buck used. Papa stands up and stretches to reach the top of the scratch marks.

"This buck is good size. If we find him, he will give us enough meat to last a while and we might get by only having to kill one more, to last the winter."

I nod in agreement.

"I think you are right. He is a big buck. Now how are we going to find him? Do you set a trap for him?" I am feeling so grown up and don't realize one does not set traps for deer.

"No, I think we are going to keep our eyes open for him and shoot him. This way we can take him back with us tonight and that will be fresh meat for now. We have more time to find another one when we come back and check the traps."

"Yes, I think that is a good idea." Hunting with Papa, I never expected this change in events. My excitement is hard to control. I must prove I am a grown up now and can be trusted to remain quiet. The problem would be keeping jabbering Timothy quiet.

"OK, lets get the mules loaded up and go up higher. The fur is thicker on the animals higher up. It is colder up there and they have to stay warm. So do we."

I pack our supplies for cooking and eating while Timothy is sitting against a fallen log and playing with twigs. He keeps tasting them and spitting them back out, then trying it again. I wonder if he expects them to taste better the next time. I carry the supplies over to Clyde and Papa ties them on to the pack. When I return, Timothy is not at the log anymore. I fear the worse and call for Papa.

He hears the frighten voice and comes running.

"Timothy was sitting right here just a minute ago. Now he is gone. Oh, Papa what if a bear got him?" I am on the verge of tears.

"Now don't get worried. Lets just look for him first. Follow his tracks."

"What tracks? He is a baby!" I couldn't believe what I am hearing.
"Look, see how the grass is broken. Lets see where it leads."
We walk about six feet and behind a bush we hear jabbering. I dash around the bush and find Timothy holding a baby rabbit upside down. He has one of its feet in his mouth tasting it. I burst out laughing and Papa comes around the bush in time to see what his son is up to.

"Well, I think my son wants to start eating meat now." Laughing, he sees me double over with laughter, holding my sides.

"We have to wait until that bunny goes up a little, son." He takes the baby and rubs grass over it so there is not human smell on it and the mother will accept it back. Then he picks up his son and gives him a hug.

"I think ye might have put a few gray hairs on your Papa's head for this stunt, not counting the fear you gave your sister. She was sure you were some bears breakfast."

Timothy, loving the excitement, laughs and pats Papa's cheeks, which makes me laugh and even Papa breaks out in a laugh.

Getting us back on Molly and secured, we continue on our way.

By dusk, all the traps have been set, and we settled down for the night. I am, exhausted, I lie down to put Timothy to sleep and fall asleep myself. Papa hearing Timothy jabbering goes and picks him up so as not to wake me, but it does.

Sitting down on the ground by the fire, he plays with Timothy, trying to wear him down so he will be willing to go to sleep. He picks up rocks and hides them in his fist and Timothy tries to get the fingers to open to get them out. He changes hands and Timothy immediately tries the other hand. This game goes back and forth and after a while Timothy rests his head against Papa's chest.

Papa begins to talk to him and tells him about our mother. Timothy, listens quietly, and soon falls to sleep. He continues to sit there, Timothy asleep in his lap, and then lays him across his criss crossed legs. He hasn't taken much time with Timothy like he did when I was a baby.

As I watch them, I wonder if it is because of Momma's death. I don't think he blames Timothy but at the same time, he has not really paid him a lot of attention like he did other boy babies on the wagon train. I can still remember him playing with me when I was little.

I know that he does not blame Timothy, or at least I think I know. Still, he makes a difference in being with Timothy then he does with me. Maybe when Timothy gets bigger they will be closer. After all, Timothy will be able to help him with outside chores while I do the women's work chores.

He picks him up and kisses him on the forehead.

"Goodnight my son. Sweet dreams." Then he slides Timothy in under the cover next to me. I wrap my arm around him, and drift off to sleep. Everything is going to be all right.

Early the next morning he smells the cooking and it wakes him up. Timothy is sitting against the log chewing on a piece of dried meat and I am finishing breakfast and serving his plate.

"About time ya get up. I thought I was going to have to load up the mules by myself." Laughing I grin real big and show him I have just served his plate with breakfast.

He goes and washes his face and then comes and sits down for prayers before we eat.

When he is done, he packs the mules and picks us up and gets us ready for the trip back down the mountain.

"Papa. When it is time to come and check the traps, will we get to come with ya?"

"I will be back in a week. I think maybe that is too soon for such a long ride. I think we will wait and see how sore ye are from riding so much. If ye are up to it, it would be my pleasure for ye to help me gather the animals and reset the traps."

Going back down the mountain, only Timothy feels like talking. Papa is deep in thought and I am already planning on what to bring on our trip next week.

About half way down, a cry brings us all alert.

"What is that?" I am looking around and up the mountain, following the rock inclines

"That is the call of a panther. It is not far away. It best we move out of its territory."

We move down hill at a faster pace and the call comes again but it is further away.

The large cat is not following us, or at least didn't sound like it is. I watch the cliffs and high rocks in case it comes back. Papa is also watching and we are going faster now.

I want to get home and be safe inside the cabin. Timothy, not afraid of anything, is playing with a twig Papa gave him, turning it this way and that, no one knowing what he finds so interesting.

As we walk around the sharp curve in the rock formation, I look down the steep drop off and can see the cabin below. Relief floods my body, knowing I am this close to home and safety and my whole body relaxes. I didn't know my muscles were so tight.

Molly and Clyde also realize home is not far away and pick up the pace. Their heads held high and their ears perked up, they have only one thing on their mind: rest, fresh food and water.

It seems to take forever to walk down to the cabin. I slide off Molly as soon as Papa takes Timothy from me. He hands Timothy back to me and I take him into the cabin. No place ever looked so good to me at this moment. I didn't realize how tired or scared I was.

Sitting Timothy down on the floor, I go to the well to get him fresh milk and hoping he will take a nap. While I am there I hear Papa talking to the mules, he is telling them what a good job they did, he rubs them down with a brown tow sack, and gives them hay. As he starts for the well, he sees me taking in the milk and some meat. I smile at him and turn and walk back to the cabin.

When he comes in he tells me for a brief moment, it was like looking at Momma, he never realized how much I look like her. He said I am growing up much too fast for my age. Maybe Mrs. Holbrook was right, we should have gone to Texas with them so I could be with children my age and go to school. He just couldn't leave Momma behind, not yet anyway. He said he was sorry but I told him that I wasn't ready to go either. I didn't want to leave Momma behind. He smiles and hugs me.

That night instead of sitting in front of the fire, he tucks me into bed and tells me a story about how he had to ask for permission to marry Momma. He said my grandparents didn't make it easy for him. My grandfather could stare a hole through a block of wood and it scared him to death. He wanted to marry Momma more though so he faced him man to man.

Turns out that Momma had already told her mother and my grandmother told my grandfather. They already knew he was coming and they were going to let him marry her. Still they pretended it was all a surprise and my grandfather made him believe he was going to say no.

Papa said he was shaking so bad, that his voice kept squeaking like a mouse. We laughed and he kissed me good night. Then he said, when the time comes for a young man to ask for my hand, he was going to be good and scare the pants off him. We laugh, he kisses me good night and I go to sleep right away. I didn't know I was so tired.

Chapter Five

Time passes and things seem to be working out. I am taking good care of Timothy and the corn is planted. I hope soon we will be going up in the mountains again. I love the trip.

One day Timothy and I take Papa his dinner in the field, with fresh cool water. It is a warm day, one of the few left before falls turns into winter. The trees are still green and heavy with leaves, although some are turning red and orange and yellow. The colors brighten up the landscape and I see beauty everywhere I look. The blackberries are thick on the vines and I have been picking them and making fried pies for Papa, something he really enjoys. Timothy just eats the berries and most of the time not only is his mouth blue but his fingers and cheeks. Soap and water just doesn't want to wash away the stains, as I scrub him several times a day. Keeping Timothy clean is getting harder and harder as he finds more things to get into.

Timothy is learning to crawl and loves to put everything in his mouth. He takes constant watching and is always getting into things. He is almost pulling himself up and Papa says it will not be long before he will be walking. I look forward to that because he is getting heavy to carry and now I must make two trips to the tree for noon meal.

As I crawl under the tree with Timothy, I encourage him to move towards the center. Then I give him something to chew on, otherwise, he will find whatever his little hands can reach and put it in his mouth. Once he is satisfied I crawl out from under the shade and carry fresh water to Papa. It is hard to walk across the fresh plowed burrows between the rows of corn, and I stumble several times. Papa is hoeing the weeds between the stalks and I can already see cobs making with a green silk showing at the top of each ear of corn.

I enjoy spending this time with Papa alone. He tells me his plans for the farm and sometimes his dreams. I believe he also enjoys these moments alone with me. He drinks some, then talks, then drinks some more. When he has had his fill, he takes my hand and we walk back to the tree.

He sometimes tells me what a fine wife and mother I will be someday from all the practicing that I am getting with Timothy.

Today, while he is drinking, a flock of wild birds suddenly take flight and fly away. They came from where the creek enters in the woods. Papa stops and listens. We hear water splashing and before I can react, Papa shouts:

"RUN, SARA, RUN! Hide under the tree and don't ye come out until I say. HURRY!"

As I run I hear him add: "Stay quiet and don't move. Keep Timothy quiet."

I run as fast as my feet will allow, frighten like I have never been before. Just as I get to the tree I look back, expecting to see him right behind me, but he is unhitching the mules, shouting at them and waving his arms, they bolt in panic.

I dive under the tree and grab Timothy. I crawl into the cavity-hiding place and hold Timothy tightly against my chest. I am rocking back and forth, shushing him; and telling him to be very quiet. He thinks we are playing with Papa and hides his face with his hands. My heart is racing and I want to close my eyes and make it all go away, but when I do I open them again so I can see when Papa comes under the tree.

I begin to shake and try as hard as I can to calm myself. I never take my eyes off the opening. Why isn't Papa coming? I realize I am holding my breath when I run out of air and have to take a gulp of air. I can hear the pounding of my heart in my ears and I can't think. I start to pray, closing my eyes and listening at the same time for Papa to come under the tree coverage. Rocking Timothy, listening and praying.

"Sh.sh.sh. Timothy, Sara's here."

I hear horses, a lot of them. I hold Timothy tighter against me, he tries to pull away but I hang on tighter and shush him. All I can say is: "Sara is with you, Sara is right here." My thoughts are asking: "Where is Papa?"

I try to look between the limbs to see if I can see Papa. I see him and he is running in the other direction. I start to call to him when I see them chasing him. One Indian falls off his horse as he swings at Papa's head with a tomahawk. They fight and I hear my father scream as he makes one last attempt to defend himself, but I see him fall to the ground.

The Indian, stands over him and cuts his throat. He holds the knife up high and screams out a loud screeching cry. The others see the blood dripping from the knife and start to hoop and holler, along with him. They chase the mules and catch them. They ride right by the tree but they can't see us and don't seem to know we are there. I am so scared that Timothy will give us away and pull him tighter to me. I try to make us part of the tree. I lean so far into the bark of the tree that it hurts my back. I hide Timothy's face in the bend of my arm so he will not make a sound. He keeps real quiet. I think he is as scared as I am. Tears slide down my face and my body starts to tremble all over. My heart is racing and it's beat is pounding in my ears. I know the slightest noise will give us away. My foot is going to sleep and I want to move it just a little to make it feel better but I don't dare. Timothy is holding onto me really tight. He starts looking around. I know he is looking for Papa.

Slowly I begin to barely rock him and hide his face again. He doesn't fight me but keeps his face hidden. I can hear the Indians talking to each other. I don't understand what they are saying so I don't know if they realize it yet that we are under the tree. I also don't know if they would kill children or not. Papa had told us the Indians were friendly. Why would they want to kill Papa? What made them angry?

I refuse to think about Papa. Right now I have to protect Timothy, even with my life. As I sit and wait I start making plans on how we can escape and then ruling them out one by one because I can also figure how or why they won't work. I know not to give up. I will never give up as long as I can take a breath.

I hear the horse's leave and the sound of the Indian's whooping as they ride away. I still do not move. One may have stayed behind to trick us. I keep Timothy close to me and slowly rock him back and forth until I feel his muscles relaxing and he rest his head against my chest. Soon, I can hear his breathing getting deeper and I know he is falling asleep. This must be his way of escaping, and for a few seconds I wish I would wake up from this dream.

Dusk falls and we are still sitting in the tree. We have food and water so we can stay hidden for a while. I strain to hear any noise that should not be out there.

Timothy sleeps soundly so I gently lay him down on the ground. Once I am sure he is sound asleep, I crawl out from under the tree. I try to see shadows that move or hear sounds that shouldn't be. I crawl on my stomach to where Papa is laying. I pray he is just playing dead and is trying to fool the Indians. I look around to see if they might have left the mules.

As I get closer I see Papa is face up in the dirt. I have been watching for hours for some movement from him but he never flinched, could he just be hurt and can't move?

I reach out and touch him and his body is hard and cold. I know now the Indians have killed him. I can see his face is covered with dry blood and when I crawl a little closer to see better in the dark, I see his throat has been cut from ear to ear. The blood has soaked the ground and the dirt is caked to his face and head. I turn around and crawl back to the tree. Anyone who would kill a man like this would kill two children who would be in their way. I must not be seen or heard and I have to protect Timothy, no matter what. As I crawl back to the tree, I must keep my stomach from churning, threatening to make me sick. I want to scream and cry out but no sound comes from my mouth. My hands are fists and I crawl back on my knees and fists like a dog would walk. I can't even think, just somehow know I have to go back to the tree. No thoughts, no tears, nothing. My mind is blank.

Just as I get to the tree and I stand up and double over. I get sick and empty my stomach. Then I look up and realize I made it back to our special tree and for a brief moment it relaxes me enough to stand upright. Looking at the tree's shadows I understand how it really is our special tree, it just saved our lives. I then realize that Timothy and I are all alone out there and fear grabs my heart and squeezes real tight, and for a brief moment I fight to get a breath. My body seems frozen and I can't move. My mind races as I just stand there staring into nothingness.

We have no neighbors or grown ups to protect us. I don't know how to hunt or kill anything. What are we going to do now? We are all alone out here. I sit down and try to think for a while. I have Timothy to think about so I have to come up with a plan and I can't make any mistakes. I have a powerful lot of thinking to do. I decide my next move has to be to talk to God.

Getting on my knees, I fold my hands together and look up at all the stars in the sky. The sky makes me feel so small and unimportant, yet I know that God is waiting to hear from me.

"Dear God; This is Sara again. Timothy and I are in a barrel full of mess. Ya, see, Papa has been killed and is on his way up there to be with Momma about now. Timothy is asleep under that tree and I am out here trying to figure out how we are going to stay alive. The way I figure it; I can't do this by myself. Since there are no more grownups around, I have to depend on you completely to tell me what to do and how to do it. Now in the Bible you spoke to Moses and gave him orders. Well, I am pretty good at obeying orders and if you will just tell me what you want me to do, I will do my darnest to do them right. See, I am not just asking for me, I have my brother who hasn't learned how to do much of anything but dirty a rag and eat yet. His life is just beginning and already he has lost his Momma and now his Papa. I am all he has left because he is too young to know anything about you yet.

Can you see the mess we are in? So, any time you decide to talk to me, just jump right in and say your peace. I am listening. Thank you. Your creation, Sara."

I stand there for a few minutes just in case He has something to say to me. Deciding He must be thinking of a plan to get us out of this mess, I crawl back under the tree and to Timothy.

Right away I realize we cannot stay out here under this tree. I have to take Timothy back to the cabin where there is food to eat and fresh milk and water. I pick him up and crawl out from under the branches. Standing up, I pick him up and he rest his head against my shoulder to go back to sleep. I start back to the cabin, then turn around and crawl back under the tree. We must wait until dark, where we will not be seen. What was I thinking to take Timothy out in the open when we could still be seen?

I have enough food to keep Timothy quiet, I hope.

When it is finally dark, really dark, I take Timothy and crawl out.

I can hear my own heartbeat, and it sounds like drums beating. I don't want to think about drums or Indians. As I walk I look up and see that the clouds are covering the moon and it gets very black. I can hardly see in front of my face and since there is no light on in the cabin, I must use my wits to get back to the cabin make sure I am going in the right direction.

I keep trying to see if I can see the mules, hoping they got away from those Indians. What would they want with mules anyway? With each step I strain to listen for sounds that shouldn't be there. Snoring, if the Indians are asleep near by, or talking, whispers or twigs snapping. Bird calls in the night because birds don't make any sounds after dark, except maybe an owl.

With each step I plan on which direction I will run if I hear or see anything. I watch for every hiding place, watching for shadows that might move or that don't belong, I even look high in the trees, in case they climbed the trees, and they are watching us high up among the branches.

I hold Timothy close to my chest, one to help keep my balance and two because I need to feel his closeness next to me for right now. He is all I have left and my reason to stay alive. He is being such a good baby, although he is wet and probably hungry again.

The only sound I hear is our hearts beating and the wind in the trees. Timothy is watching also, holding tightly to my hair with one hand and his thumb in his mouth with the other hand. I don't know if it is to keep him quiet or if he is just scared. I just know he has never sucked his thumb before now.

I have to force myself to take each step. I make myself to take four steps and then tell myself how brave I am and to do it again. I don't feel brave; in fact, I ain't never been so scared in my whole life.

What if being out here gets us killed or worse get taken to where they live. Will they skin us alive? Or tie us to a tree and set fire to us? Will they kill Timmy in front of me?

"STOP IT!!! YOU'RE ONLY SCARING YOURSELF. THIS IS THE TIME TO BE BRAVE, YOU HAVE A BABY TO PROTECT AND YA CAN'T DO IT BY MAKING YOURSELF SCARED. NOW STRAIGHTEN UP AND FLY RIGHT!" I fuss at myself, giving me the talk I need to hear to do what I gotta do. I sure don't feel brave, but I am alive and I intend to stay that way and to keep my brother alive too.

It seems to take forever for us to reach the cabin. As I start up the steps I stop. What if the Indians are in the cabin and waiting for us? How will I know if it is a trap or not?

I carefully tiptoe up the side steps, keeping my back to the wall. I slowly step over to one of the windows and look in. They have been there but they seem to be gone now. Everything in the cabin is destroyed and lying scattered all over the floor. The cabin looks a mess. If it looks this bad in the dark, what is it going to look like in the morning, in the light? I finally reach the door and stop. What if they are still in there and hiding, knowing someone will return to the cabin? They don't know that Momma is gone, or we are still here.

Taking a deep breath, I slowly step through the doorway and then begin to step-over the things that are scattered all over the floor. The bed is turned upside down, dishes are broken and scattered all over the floor. Timothy's crate is finally found and I make him a soft bed and lay him down in it. At first he starts to fuss then he stops and rolls over and sticking his thumb in his mouth, goes back to sleep.

This gives me time to look around. I can't help but wonder if I will ever be able to make this a home again for Timothy and me. I will just have to try. I don't see where I have any choice. I sure can't try to walk away from the cabin, to go looking for other people; I might just walk right into their camp. Besides, I don't have any idea which direction to go. What if the Indians have destroyed the town that Papa sometimes went to? What direction is this town? He never took me on these trips, I had to stay home and help Momma with the chores because she was with Timothy in her belly.

Timothy is going to wake up hungry. Do I dare try to make it to the well and get some milk? What if they are out there watching the house?

If I don't at least try, his crying is going to attract attention and bring the Indians to the front door. I can't risk him crying, I have to go back outside and go to the well for the milk.

Darn if I ain't just plum scared out of my britches. I don't want to go. I don't want to stay and have Timothy wake up hungry and crying. I don't see where I have a choice.

Making my way to the door, I stop, frozen in place with only the pounding of my heart to hear. I barely stick my head out the door. I really do not want to go back outside. What if they are out there waiting for me in the dark? Will they scalp me or stab me? What will they do to Timothy? I turn my back against the door, shaking.

"I can't do this. This is just too much for a little girl to have to do. This is not right. I am ready to wake up now from this nightmare." I bang my head against the door and feel its unyielding bump against my head.

SARA'S VOW

Nothing happens and I know I am living this nightmare for real. I am determined to protect my brother, and keeping my vow. Pushing my back against the wall, I side step to the right and around the corner and then to the well, being very careful to stay in the shadows of the cabin. I listen for sounds that should not be there. I realize I am holding my breath when I run out of air and have to gasp for a breath.

Squatting down in the well's shadows I can't believe I am doing this. Nothing has ever prepared me for this. Parents are not suppose die and leave their children behind, unprotected. Now, I understand why Papa wanted to go back east after Momma went away. There would be more people to help take care of us and maybe he would still be alive.

I pull myself up to the well, looking all around. When I am satisfied that no one is there, I pull the bucket up by hand, instead of using the pulley. The pulley squeaks and I don't want to make any sounds. The milk is still there and so is the meat. The Indians didn't find it. I remove the milk and some of the meat and lower the bucket slowly back into the well. When it hits the water, it makes a little splash; I then tie the rope to keep it from falling into the well and then sit back down. I am tempted to get a drink of the milk but don't dare. It might be all there is, if the Indians killed the goat or stole her. That is when I realize I have not heard the goat call for her food or milking, so I have to save all the milk for Timothy.

Taking a deep breath, I have to force myself to get up the nerve to try to make it back into the cabin. I really want to just stay there and hide until I wake up. I must be having a nightmare and any time now Papa will be waking me up. As I sit there, holding tightly to the milk and meat, I know it is not just a nightmare but a real life nightmare that I am living. I make myself stand up and taking one small step at a time, with my back against the outside wall, I force myself take just one step then another until I reach the porch.

Peering around the corner and looking for moving shadows and seeing none, I step up on the porch. I continue to keep my back pressed against the cabin and side step, closing the shutters as I go, until I am once again inside the cabin. I make a quick glance around the cabin to be sure we are still alone. With great relief, I go to the sink and sit the milk and meat down, turn and see that Timothy is still sleeping. Oh to be a baby again. I go to the chimney and feel for Papa's rifle but it is gone. The Indians must have taken it.

Next, I check the kitchen shelves and find a long knife. Sitting down next to Timothy, I wait for the Indians to break their way back into the cabin. I try to plan what to do but I ain't sure if any of the plans I make will work out. The one thing I am sure about is that I must protect Timothy. Sitting with the knife in my hands, I rest my head against the wall and wait. My eyelids start to get heavy and I must fight sleep, I have to stay awake.

I must have dozed off because I waken to hear Timothy calling. I manage to crawl to him and hold him, reassuring him that I am there. He is soaked and I crawl around searching for a rag and change him, then take the corner of a piece of cloth and dip it in the milk on it just like Mrs. Holbrook had shown me. I feed him until I can feel his tummy being tight. It is the only way I know for sure he is full; otherwise, he will keep drinking until he gets a tummy ache and then he cries. I can't have him bawling right now.

Still, sitting on the floor, hiding, I hum a tune and rock him back to sleep. I know he is exhausted. He has never been awake so much during the night like he was last night. As he sleeps, I brush his fine hair away from his face with my fingers and whisper to him, telling him what a wonderful baby he is. As I talk to him, I start calling him Timmy, my own special name for him now. I sit and rock him, holding him close to me. We only have each other now.

It is pitch dark in the cabin so I gently lay Timmy back in his crate and start to crawl around on my hands and knees, feeling in every nook and cranny as I look for a lantern. I find one, still unbroken, behind Momma and Papa's bed frame, but the light will shine through the windows and might draw the Indians attention to the cabin. I keep crawling around, looking for what ever scrap I can find to put over the windows, and to block all holes, even the tiniest ones, before I can start cleaning up the mess the Indians made.

Tonight I will work with the dimness of a lantern with the smallest light possible.

"This is our home and it is up to me to make things as normal as possible for Timmy's sake. I am not going to be able to sleep, anyway, and I want to put things back in order. It is what I should do, Momma would want me to do it." I whisper to myself, maybe to keep me from feeling so alone and to make me feel stronger. Whatever the reason it works.

The stillness and soundlessness from outside, many times causing me to feel someone else is in the room with us. Fear grips my heart and squeezes. I can't get my breath. I stand frozen with fear, as I try to see the Indian standing right in front of me. I think about running out the door, but the rest could be out there waiting, or he could run and catch me and then kill me. Then I remember my brother is sleeping in his crate and I know I can't leave. I have to protect Timmy.

I can't control my fear, I see a shadow standing very still and I know we are not alone in the cabin. I try to take a deep breath, but it comes in small spurts of air as every muscle tightens. I can't think, I can't move. I just stand there and stare at the shadow, watching/waiting for it to come and kill me.

Finally I gather the nerve to face the Indian in the corner, I slowly move my foot forward, just a tiny bit, more of a scoot then a step.

When he doesn't move, I breathe in and slowly out again. I can do this. I must do this. I find the nerve to walk towards him. I force my feet to move forward then finally taking another deep breath I reach out to touch him, my hand is shaking so hard I can see it shivering in the dimness of what moonlight is coming in through the cracks of the shutters.

To my much relief, I discover it is Papa's shirt hanging on a nail. I almost burst out laughing but I don't want to wake Timmy. I have to put my hands over my mouth to keep quiet and hold my giggles in.

After a time or two of these little scares, I realize I am allowing my thoughts to scare me and my imagination is running wild. I crawl over and move what ever I think is an Indian and then fuss at myself for being such a baby.

All during the night, every time I pass a window, I look outside, trying to see a shadow that shouldn't be there or hear a sound that doesn't sound quite right. I search in all directions, as far as I can see. I tiptoe about the cabin, not only to not wake Timmy but so I can hear if anyone or anything steps up on the porch. Just a wrong step and one of the boards will creak. I want be so sure that if any trouble is about to happen and I will be prepared. I put knives up high in various parts of the cabin. I also hide matches where I can find them if I need to get to them in a hurry. I hang blankets and shirts and even Papa's coat over the windows to block out any of the light from inside.

Next I look under the bed to see what might be under there that I can use and find Papa's gun. I crawl over and set it by the front door. I open a crate where he kept a good supply of shells and put a box on the windowsill next to the door. Having the gun gave me a feeling that I am now in control of what ever may happen. They won't expect a girl to be shooting at them. I don't know if they will come back but if they do I am prepared to go down fighting if I must.

I talk to Momma and tell her Papa is coming her way. I talk to Papa and tell him not to worry that I will take good care of my brother. I talk to God and ask Him to keep an eye on us and to warn us of danger. I even talk to myself, going over every little detail to protect us.

I am scared and admit it. I am too young to be left all alone with a baby to protect. I just turned seven a few days ago, the way I figure it, and there has been nothing in my life to get me ready for this. I talk to myself because I need to have someone to tell me what to do and give me strength. Someone who believes I can do anything. I am just not so sure I am the one to be telling me I can do this.

Sometime during the night I step outside. Staying in the shadows and against the wall, I side step all the way around the cabin. When

I reach an area that the moon is shining, I dash to the next dark spot. By the time I make it back to the front porch, I feel confident that we are alone and the Indians have left, at least for now.

I check on Timmy, he is still sleeping soundly, like nothing has happened. I scoot his box over by the corner and hide it behind some boxes and a chair covered with a quilt. He can't be seen. Now if he will just stay asleep and quiet, I can do what I know needs to be done next.

I find Papa's shovel and walk up the hill, next to Momma's grave. I know it has to be longer and wider than Momma's. I remember when I stood on my tiptoes and stretched out my hands up high, I still couldn't reach his shoulders. So I lie down and stretch my toes back as far as I can and move them back and forth to make a mark in the dirt, then I reach above my head and make a mark with the tip of my fingers. I get up and walk to the mark and try to figure, how big his head and neck are and make another mark. Just to be sure I have it long enough I make another mark several hand lengths further. If I dig the hole this long, it should be long enough for Papa.

Then I begin to dig around the area from one end to the other so I can see in the dark where I need to dig. Standing and stretching my back, I look down. I never thought I would be digging a grave for Papa. I tell myself I can do this; I just have to set my mind to do it and then do it. That's what Papa always said when he had to do something he didn't want to do.

I dig and dig and shovel the dirt out of the hole, then step forward, and dig some more. There are rocks under the dirt and I have to dig them out and set them aside. I could use his pick but it is too heavy for me to lift over my head and swing it down hard on the rocks. I just have to make do with what I can work with. Even though it makes it a lot harder. I work from the foot area to the head and then back to the foot area. I have a nice pile of dirt all around the hole and my body aches something awful. I stand up straight and rub my back and look at how far I have come and realize the hole is not deep enough to bury a dog in. I hang my head. I know it is long enough but how long is it going to take me to dig it deep enough? Then I get angry, very angry.

"I shouldn't have to do this! This is not right for a child to have to dig her Papa's grave. Why did we ever come to this land in the first place? Why couldn't Papa just leave with the Holbrooks? We could be on our way to Texas and safe and together." The more I fuss the harder I stomp on the shovel and the deeper it goes into the dirt. Each time I fill the shovel and throw the dirt out of the hole, I come up with another reason why this just isn't right. I clinch my jaw, and put all I have into the digging. When I can't grip the handle anymore I stop. I crawl out of the hole and look down into it. It seems to be pretty deep but Papa is a big man and will take up a lot of room. I am so tired I almost fall back into the hole. I back away a couple of steps.

"It will just have to do for now. If I need to dig more it will be after I get Papa up that hill. Now that is another problem I will have to face after I check on Timothy." Talking to myself seems to help. I start down the hill, and look up and ask God:

"How am I going to take care of Timmy all by myself? I am not even old enough to take care of myself. I can't take him back east, or take him west. I wouldn't even know how to go about setting out in either direction. I might walk right into the Indian camp. I wish we had neighbors or a town close by. Surely there must be some people somewhere about. It feels like Timmy and I are the only ones in this valley."

The more I think about what an impossible life I have right now, the more I cry, which really makes me angry.

"My hands hurt, my back hurts and I have no one to hold me and tell me everything is going to be better. Papa planted the corn, but I don't know how to take care of it. I don't know how to harvest it, and there is no one to teach me."

My hands burn and although it is too dark and my hands are too dirty to see anything, I know I have blisters that have popped and the skin is torn by the way they sting.

SARA'S VOW

Timmy will be waking up soon and wanting his milk. As I get closer to the cabin I hear the nanny goat calling me. She has spotted me. Now she wants her feed and to be milked. I feel tuckered out and just want to lie down for a while but the goat's baying could get the Indians attention and they might come back. I don't see where I have any choice. Before I can rest I must milk the goat.

I quickly check on Timmy and he is still sleeping soundly, like nothing has happened. This is good. I don't know what I would do if he starts crying and calling for Papa right now.

I wash my hands, get the bucket and head for the corral to milk that darn goat. As I walk, staying in the shadows and running from one cover area to the next, I watch for moving shadows or sounds that should not be there. I move quietly and make sure I don't kick any rocks or step on any sticks that will break and make a noise.

While I am milking the goat, I think about the grave I have been digging. What if it is not deep enough? The wild animals will smell Papa and dig him up and eat on him. I can't have that happen. If the animals are big enough they might even carry him off into the woods to eat him. The worse would be if they dug him up and were eating on him right on his grave or near by. I have to fix the grave where they can't get to him.

Then, as if a voice in my head spoke to me, I understand what I need to do. All I have to do is carry enough large stones to cover the grave and make them several stones high, maybe knee high and then the animals cannot dig him up.

I look around and see a lot of stones, some are bigger than others but enough to cover the grave real good and still have some left over. It is going to take a while to get all these stones up the hill, but they ain't going no where and I have a lot of time on my hands, my whole life. We can't go no where either, we are stuck here just like those stones.

Then I hear hooves beating against the earth. INDIANS!!! Timothy is in the house by himself and I am way out in the barn. If I dart for the cabin, they will find Timothy, but if they see me running away they will chase me. I start racing for the woods then turn and race for the cabin.

"I can't leave Timmy alone and behind. What ever happens we will be together."

I drop the milk bucket and run as fast as my legs will carry me towards the cabin. Just as I jump for the porch, Molly runs up to the hitching post and stops. She has somehow gotten away from the Indians and come home.

I stop short and stare, not believing my eyes at first, then jumping off the porch and running and putting my arms around the mule's neck, hugging my lost friend.

"Papa always said God never made a more stubborn mule than you or smarter. I bet you taught those Indians a thing or two before you left too, didn't you? I am so happy you come home. I didn't know what I was going to do but now I have you."

I hear Timmy waking up and go inside to get him. He sees me and wants to go outside too. I change his rag and pick him up. As soon as he sees Molly he begins to squirm, wanting to pet her. I walk to the hitching post and let him pat her neck over and over again and Molly just stands there and takes it, as if she understands he is just a baby. Timmy squeals with delight and pulls on her mane and rubs his face against her neck. She raises her head, perhaps proudly, as if expecting all this excitement from her coming home.

As we stand there, the sun starts to rise and the first rays of a new day appear, God's promise that He will always be with us.

I take Timmy back inside and break a piece of dried meat and give it to him to suck on and put him back in the crate. I watch him chewing and sucking on the meat, the juices run down his chin. He will need a bath when he is worn out from all the sucking and chewing. Now that he is happy I need to go outside to take care of Molly and finish milking.

Taking a hold of the broken rope that is around her neck, I lead her to the well, and draw up a fresh bucket of water for her to drink. When she drinks her fill, I walk with her to the barn, where I throw in some dried cut grass and close the gate. Molly immediately starts to eat and I return to the milking that I was doing before all the excitement started.

As I milk, I press my head against the goat's side and talk to the goat.

"Just when a person starts to think everything has gone wrong, things change, the sun comes up with a bright new day and things look better. I am not saying everything is back to the way it was, it will never be that way again, I am just saying, maybe Timmy and I can make it out here by ourselves with your and Molly's help. I didn't know if the Indians found you last night or not. It was your hollering that told me you were safe and sound. Timmy would not make it if you were gone. I am mighty grateful that for once in your life you kept quiet long enough for those Indians to leave. Yep, things are looking better for us. Who knows, maybe some people will move close by and come visit sometimes. Maybe they might even have a boy goat for you to marry and you can have another baby. That wouldn't be so bad. There, all done. I thank you kindly for your milk, Timmy needs it and it fills his belly."

Standing I rub the goat on the neck and pat her behind and walk out carrying the bucket with fresh milk. Now all I have to do is strain it and put it in a jar and put the jar in the bucket and lower it into the well to keep cool. That's easy work.

I go back to the cabin and feed Timmy again until his belly is tight. I bathe him and put on a clean rag and then lay him down in the crate and start singing to him. It doesn't take long before he falls back to sleep.

I know I have more work to do and with him sleeping, now is the best time to do it. I head around back, to the barn, to get Molly. Tying an extra rope on her, I lead her to the field where Papa is still waiting for me to come and get him buried.

I have given this a lot of thought, all night in fact, and now with Molly back, it is going to be a lot easier for me. I have it figured out in my mind. Now if things will just go as I planned, I will have this done before

Timmy wakes up again. He doesn't sleep as much as he use to. I think he is afraid he is going to miss something and sleeps just long enough to give his tummy a chance to rest and then he is raring to go again. He stays awake longer now too.

I walk Molly to the field. Next I turn her around and back her up closer to Papa. I take the rope and tie Papa's feet together. Then I tie the rope to Molly. I sure do wish I could lift him to the buckboard like he did with Momma, but he is too heavy. This is the only way to get him up the hill to the grave.

Leading Molly, I walk slowly and we drag Papa across the field that he had cleared with his bare hands and plowed with the help of the mules. We pass in front of the cabin that Papa built and I remember how he talked about adding two more bedrooms for Timmy and me some day. We walk past the well he dug with just a shovel, and then rocked the inside so the water would be clear. He climbed up and down the rope to do this. We lowered the rocks down in the bucket. It was a lot of weight but Momma and I handled it just fine.

Remembering these bits and pieces helps me not think what I am having to do right now and what I will have to do when we get to the top of the hill.

We finally start up the hill where Momma is and his grave is waiting for him. I keep talking to Molly so she doesn't get spooked and take off running with Papa following behind. Molly, being a smart mule, seems to understand and listens to my talking. She walks slowly and does not misbehave. My knots are weak and come untied a bunch of times, then I have to stop Molly and retie the knots. Eventually we make it up the hill.

I refuse to look at Papa's head and concentrate only on his feet. However, now we are at the grave, I must face my fears and get him into the hole I spent the night digging. His face is worse than I remember from last night, now it is swollen and all black and blue with the slashes cut deep into his forehead and jaw. I turn away and then straighten my back and tell myself there is a job to do and I am going to do it.

Moving Molly as close to the grave hole as she will walk, I guide her until Papa is even with the grave. I tell Molly to stand and start to untie the ropes, but they have tightened from the weight and the pulling so I have to sit down and work on untying the knots. Refusing to look at Papa again, eventually I get the knots undone and free Papa's feet and Molly.

The way I figured it, I could just scoot Papa over and into the grave, but that doesn't happen. When I am pushing to move him over, he rolls and goes into the grave face down!

Molly spooks at the grave, raising her front feet and trying to back away. I quickly grab the rope and hold on tight. Speaking firming but not in a panic voice, I finally calm Molly and tie her to a tree further away from the grave. I rub her neck and around her long ears and speak softly to her, and she settles right down.

Going back to the grave, I look at Papa's back towards the sky and him facing down. I don't know if it makes much difference but it didn't seem right to bury him face down. He is tight against the dirt in some places and in some places he has some extra room. I have to at least try to make it right.

Looking back at Molly, I know she will never help me get him turned over. She has done her part and she has had enough and wants no part of the grave or body anymore. Looking at Molly and then at the grave I know it is up to me to get Papa rolled over and face up.

"Well I am going to need some help." I say out loud. Looking up, I get on my hands and knees and say a prayer. Then I crawl into the grave with Papa.

Grabbing his arm and putting my feet against the wall of the grave, on the opposite side, I put my back to the grave's wall and with all my might I push to straighten my knees and using my strength to pull Papa over on his side. He rolls just a little bit but he did move some, this lets me know I can do this. I just have to keep trying. I reposition myself and try again. I jerk and pull and grab his pants at the waist and pull and he moves a little bit more. I grab his leg and try to roll it over his other leg but it keeps falling back.

I change positions and get on the other side of him and put my back against the grave wall and place my bare feet against him. I am wedged in tight with my knees bent and almost touching my chin. I push against the grave wall with my back and my feet against Papa. He rolls over but his arm is now under him. Now I have a powerful hard time getting that arm out from under him. I have to crawl over him and wedging my feet against the grave on both sides. I tug on the arm and pull right and left and right and left and up until it finally comes free and I fall back and sit on Papa. Now he is on his side. That's half way.

I climb out of the grave and look at Papa. As I stare down at Papa, in my mind, I work out different ways to go about getting him to scoot over so I can roll him over on his back and have his face up.

"This sure would be a lot easier if Molly wasn't so darn scared. Heck he is dead, he can't do anything to her." I straighten and bend side to side to loosen those muscles that are strained and tired. A soft bed sure would feel good right now, but not until the work is done.

The sun is high in the sky and I know Timmy will be waking soon if not already. He'll want something to eat and his rag changed, he might even be crying now. I start back down the hill with Molly and tie her to the hitching post while I go into the cabin to check on Timmy.

Timmy is awake and playing with his rag. How he got it off I don't know but now he needs a bath really bad. So I get some water and begin to clean him. I am still afraid to build a fire, the smoke might alert the Indians so he is just going to have to deal with the water being colder than he likes.

He screams and cries and doesn't enjoy the bath one bit. I am also not happy, now I am soaking wet and still have to finish the job on top of the hill.

I give Timmy the doll that Momma had made when she was still big with Timmy. He loves playing with it and chewing on the cloth. I lay him back in his now clean crate and walk back up the hill. While walking up, I start thinking about how I am going to get Papa on his back.

Once again I brace my feet on the opposite walls, and lift his shoulder up and then push with my feet and his body actually moves just a little. Next, I grab his waistband and taking the same position, try to move him again. This must be a heavier part for he didn't move at all.

So I stand over him and lifting him up and down just a little. I bounce him and pull him over to the other side. IT WORKS. Now I move his bottom leg over. This is more difficult because he has the top leg weighing the bottom leg down. I use the shovel handle to help pry it over. Bit by bit I get the leg to move. Once it is where it needs to be, I pull the top leg over.

Next, I climb into the grave and bracing my back against the wall, I put my feet against Papa tummy and shove with all my might and he rolls over some more.

I work on getting him to scoot over one body part at a time and finally have him face up. I am exhausted but at least he is face up.

I lie down beside the grave and take a deep breath. Looking up at the clouds I make images with my mind and slowly my muscles relax and my breathing returns to normal.

I look up and realize the sun is half way down to sunset and I must go back to the cabin to check on Timmy.

Timmy is playing quietly with the rag I had on him. The rag is dry but his bedding is soaked. I take Timmy out and put the rag back on him and sit him on Papa and Mommas bed. Then I take out the bedding and put fresh bedding in the crate, fussing at the same time at Timmy.

"I don't understand why you think you must take your rag off all the time. You just make a mess of your bed. Besides you can't go around naked, it just ain't right."

He doesn't understand what I am saying or listens; instead he just jabbers right back at me.

This time I take Timmy up the hill with me. I can keep a better eye on him if I can see him. I take a couple of his favorite toys and sit him down under the tree while I go back to the grave.

I pick up the shovel and realize the blisters are awfully tender. I begin shoveling the dirt back in. Trying very hard not to look as the dirt hits Papa. I talk to Timmy and shovel as fast as I can until I can no longer see anything of Papa. Then I sit down, and with my feet, I shove the fresh dirt into the grave. My hands are bleeding and raw from using the shovel. They will heal in time.

Timmy crawls over and I am surprised to see him next to me. He has never crawled before. Then I understand he hasn't because I am always carrying him. I keep shoving the dirt on top of the grave wanting to get this over with so I can start concentrating on making a home for Timmy and me. All I have to do now is put the rocks on top of the grave.

No time like the present, I force myself to stand up and start gathering as big of rocks that I can carry and place them gently on the grave. Once I have a layer that covers the whole grave, I start on the second layer. I continue with layers until I have at least four or five layers. Then I stand back and look at the grave. I make sure that I can't see any fresh dirt. I must be sure that the animals will not bother Papa's grave. Now all that is left is to make a cross and carve his name on it and plant it at the head of the grave, like he did for Momma. I can start on that tomorrow.

Picking up Timmy, I move him to my hip, because he is easier to carry that way. He grabs one of my ears to hang onto and we go back down the hill. The hard work is done and now all I have to do is figure out how we are going to survive. I don't have any ideas coming to my mind yet but I know God will give me the answers as soon as I need them. I begin singing Jesus Loves The Little Children, and smile as I march to the beat of the song. I just know we are going to be all right, I feel it inside.

The next morning, I gather the bucket and turn to look at Timmy, who is already awake and ready to get into what ever he can find.

"Well, since you are crawling now, I can't leave you alone in the cabin. So, how about you coming with me while I go and milk the goat?" Picking him up, I walk out of the cabin and around the side of the house. The goat has gotten loose and is in the cut grass bin. I have to run so I sit Timmy on the ground, grab the goat and by her horns, walking backwards pulling her back to her stall.

"You're a bad goat. Why did you go into the cut grass bin? You had plenty right here. Look at all this grass I left you. Bad Girl. Now you will stay here all night and maybe after your morning milking tomorrow I will forgive you and stake you where you can get some green grass and weeds." I get my stool, sit down and start and milking the goat. With the excitement I blum forgot I have Timmy in the barn with me.

I take the milk back to the cabin and strain it and then take it to the well. While I am lowering it into the well, I glance over and see Timmy hanging onto Molly's front leg and he is standing there holding on for dear life. I can see his tiny legs trying to buckle and I know if Molly moves that foot, Timmy could get hurt really bad. I also know I can't shout or run over there because it might spook Molly and Timmy could be stepped on.

With my heart racing I tie the rope, as quickly as I can, with the bucket still hanging in the air. Taking a deep breath, I turn and walk calmly, although I didn't feel a bit calm, and go into the stall and pick up Timmy, who burst into laughter and Molly points her ears forward as if to say, "You need to be more careful with your colt."

"What a big boy you are, and YOU MOLLY, what a wonderful Mule you are." I rub Molly's ears and gently kiss her cheek. She closes her eyes for just a second and I know she understands the kiss was my way of saying thank you.

I march back with Timmy to the cabin and put him in the crate and then closing the cabin door, return to give Molly an extra helping of cut grass, and fresh water from the well. Molly seem to know she is being rewarded and rubs her head against me several times, wanting to be petted even more. Maybe she thinks I will give her another kiss, which I do as I leave.

I return to the cabin, only to find Timmy not in his crate. I know he can't get out of the cabin, so I start searching for him, calling him. Down on my hands and knees I crawl around, looking under Momma and Papa's bed and behind crates and chairs and Timmy is no where to be found. Standing to get a better view I look again. He is not jabbering or making any sounds and I am stumped as to where he can be. He started scooting like a worm, just days before. Now he has scooted to heaven only knows where inside the cabin.

Finally, I decide I am going to trick him and decide to take out one of Momma's pots and a wooden spoon and beat on the pan with the spoon. Timmy loves anything that makes noise and this will bring him out of his hiding place. Smiling I walk over to the counter and pull back the curtain, only to find Timmy asleep under the counter, with his head on the floor and the wooden spoon in his hand, and his leg propped up and over the pan.

It is all I can do to keep from bursting out laughing. He is such a funny sight.

Seems he has been watching and knew where the noisemaker is kept. I very gently pick him up and tiptoe to Papa's bed where I slowly lay him down. For the first time, Timmy and I sleep on Momma and Papa's bed. I didn't mean to sleep all evening and night. I guess I didn't realize just how tuckered I was. Whatever the reason, I feel refreshed and ready for a new day to begin when I wake up.

Timmy wakes me up with pulling my hair. Neither one of us had eaten supper the night before. He is hungry and it is past time for breakfast. I get him a clean rag and put it on him and then go outside to get the milk and meat. When I go to pull up the bucket, my head begins to spin and I sit down with the rope still held tightly in my hand. I am having trouble seeing. Everything seems blurry. I rest my head back against the rock well wall and close my eyes.

It is then I realize I haven't eaten since the picnic under the tree with Papa. I fed Timmy but never thought about eating myself. Now I am hungry.

This is when I begin to understand that in order to be able to take care of Timmy I must take care of myself. If anything happens to me, Timmy will not survive. I have to do what Papa and Momma did just so we will survive.

I look up on the hill and try to see the graves. I miss them something terrible, but they are gone forever. We are all alone and winter is coming. There is no time for crying anymore. I must remember what they did to survive. More determined than I have ever been, I turn around and hanging onto the well's rocks, I pull myself up to a standing position. I look up the mountain and remember Papa's traps. That's fresh meat that we can eat.

Can I remember where the traps are? I decide today is the day I am going to try. I will have to take Timmy with me and we will ride Molly and find at least some of those traps and maybe get fresh meat to eat, and furs for drying to make winter clothes. I will need to reset the traps also. I will have to leave some meat in the traps from the animals I catch.

Excited that I have a plan, I feel very grown up. I have a baby to take care of and one day he will be old enough to help me. We are going to make it. We are survivors. I think that is the word Papa used on the boat when so many people got sick.

I take the milk and meat into the cabin and sit and eat with Timmy. Telling Timmy what my plans are. I feel full of energy and just know now we can make it. All I have to do is remember where the traps are, figure out how to reset them, and pray we don't run into some bear or wolf that wants the meat as much as we do, and not get lost and wander in the Indian camp. That stops me in my tracks. I can't take a chance on running into those Indians. Most Indians are supposed to be friendly, at least that is what the town folks told Papa when he stopped to pay for the land. Said not to worry. They were wrong.

I gather the corn instead and stack it beside the cabin. I shuck a couple of ears and boil it and then scrap it off the cob so Timmy can eat it. It taste good and it fills our tummies. At least we can go to bed with full stomachs.

Later as Timmy sleeps, I sit on the porch and get to thinking about the day that Johnny was here. I smile at the playing we did in the creek, and laugh at myself for believing all those gold rocks was really gold. Too bad it wasn't. Still they are pretty rocks and in daylight I can still see the piles we made.

That's when I know what I can do with those rocks. I will haul them up to the graves and put them on Momma and Papa's graves. They don't have no fancy tombstones like they have in the big cities, just simple crosses with their names carved in them from one of the kitchen knives, but now they can have mighty fancy graves.

Right after breakfast the next morning I start carrying my skirt full of the small stones and hauling them up the hill to the graves. With skirt full after skirt full, I climb the hill and dump the stones on the graves. Each time I smile and run back for another load.

By the time Timmy wakes up, Momma's grave is shining a golden glow. I rest while I feed Timmy and then show him what I am doing. He claps his hands and laughs. Sometimes I wonder if he understands, and then decide probably not, just happy, as usual, that I am talking to him.

When Timmy goes to sleep for his afternoon nap, I start on Papa's grave. I can't do much for my folks but I can do this. With each load I can see the difference and I just know my parents are watching me and laughing with me. I can feel inside that they are proud of me.

The more I think about them watching me, the more energy I seem to have. For the first time since Papa died I am truly happy inside. Their graves are going to be the prettiest graves in the whole world. No one will have such a pretty grave.

By the time I remember we were suppose to go and find the traps it is too late. We will just have to do it tomorrow. One more day won't make any difference.

Chapter Six

    I milk the goat and bridle Molly, and then I dress Timmy in double sets of clothes and pack rags to take with us. I add a damp rag for washing him if he gets dirty. I get Papa's canteen and fill it with fresh water. Stuff a feed sack with small hand ropes for tying the animals on Molly. I pick up Timmy and walk out and close the door. There is no lock because we never needed one. I put Timmy on Molly and lead her to the fence, where I climb up the post and slide my leg over on Molly's back, behind Timmy, and then grabbing the saddle horn I scoot over and get comfortable.
    Now all I have to do is ride Molly up the mountain and find those traps, nothing to it.
    I look back at the cabin as we ride up the mountain, I thought I felt alone before, at least I had the cabin and food and water and milk down there. Now I must watch the weather signs and keep my eyes open for shelter if it turns bad, watch for bears and wild Indians. I start to feel scared and think about turning around. I glance back behind us and wonder if I am leading us into more trouble. I gotta stop thinking this way. I turn back and face ahead. Molly walks on. To go back would be slowly starving to death. If we have to, better to die fast then slow.
    I think about my surroundings. Watching trees and rock formations so as to remember when I come back this way. I have to be careful not to get us lost up here with no shelter. I wonder what I was thinking about taking Timmy out here with me. I couldn't leave him behind but I must have been plum crazy to bring him out here alone with only me

to protect him. What ever got into my head? Well, what's done is done. I will just have to make the best of it and be careful and watchful like Papa taught me. I can do this. I have to do this.

Soon the fear is gone as I begin to recognize different things Papa had pointed out to me on our trip. Now I know I am on the correct trail.

"See Timmy, over there is where Papa showed me he killed a big buck last year. I know we are going right. It won't be long now before we start finding the traps."

We go a ways further and I stop Molly. Sliding off, I take Timmy off the mule and set him down by a boulder. Next, I duck under the low limbs of a tall pine, next to the trunk is a dead rabbit, caught in one of Papa's traps. He ain't been dead too long because he is still limp.

I go back to Molly and take off the piece of iron Papa had said to use. He showed me how to open the trap and reset it. To free the rabbit would be the same way. Sticking the iron bar into the trap, I shove open the teeth and step on a lever that keeps it open. Reaching down I take the rabbit and toss it aside, then reset the trap. Slowly, I let off my foot and remove the bar. The trap stays set. Smiling I pick up the rabbit by its ears and take it back to Molly. I tie the back feet to a small rope on the saddle, and then return to pick up Timmy.

"We are going to be all right. We will have meat to eat and you will have milk to drink. Soon I will figure out how to make corn meal for cornbread and come up with some way to save the rest of the corn. I will have to save enough for planting next year, too.

You will see I am going to take good care of you. You don't have to worry about that." I pick him up and sit him on the saddle. He is holding onto the saddle horn and I climb up a big rock and stretch my right leg across Molly as I slide over onto her back, behind Timmy.

Wrapping my arms around him, I take the reins and gently kick Molly. Molly slowly steps forward and returns to the trail she knows so well. I sit tall behind the saddle; confident I will be able to take care of Timmy thru the winter.

We follow the trail that Papa used to set the traps. I may have missed a couple but by high sun we had several rabbits, a fox, a raccoon, and fish that were caught in a trap that looked like a cone on the inside. The fish would swim in through the big hole and out the smaller hole at the other end, which is closed but has enough room for the fish to swim, there they would stay, not knowing how to swim back out. I reset all the traps for the next time we come and we head for home.

Molly never misses a step. She knows exactly which bend that will take us back home and I never doubt her judgment.

Once back in our valley, I ride Molly to the barn. I slide off and then take Timmy and sit him in the grass bin. I remove the saddle and the animals, then the bridle. Molly goes to get a drink, and I throw the animals over my shoulder like Papa use to do. Next, I bend down and pick up Timmy. Together, they make a heavy load, but I am determined to get them into the cabin in one trip. I count my steps, telling myself to take just five more steps, then five more until I reach the front porch.

I am tired and need to change Timmy and then feed him. Next, I have to gut the animals and wash them and skin the hides. Then I will scrap the hides and nail them to the barn wall for them to dry. My day will not end anytime soon.

As I walk into the cabin, I am shocked to see someone has been there and turned everything upside down. INDIANS. They came back. I sit Timmy down and throw the animals in the bucket. I find Timmy's crate and put back his blanket and sit him in it. Papa's and Momma's bed is on its side. I strain as I get it to roll back over on all four legs.

Now I head for the well, and the milk is gone, as is what little meat that was left. Thank God I saw the goat behind the barn, she will still be able to give milk for Timmy.

Straightening my back, I put my hands on my hips, I set my jaw and think out loud:

"Momma always said a woman's work is never done. I didn't

know what she meant but I do now." I take the bucket and put the animals in the sink, then, I go to the well and wash the bucket out. Next I march behind the barn and kneel down and milk the goat.

"I just don't know why those Indians won't leave us alone. Maybe now they will think they killed everyone and will go back to where ever they came from. Now I can't cook anything because they might smell the smoke and come back. They took the dried meat. Looks like I will just have to drink goats milk tonight too for my supper." I fuss while I milk the goat. Standing up I pat the goat and rub between her horns. Then smiling I bend over and kiss the goat on the forehead.

"I thank ya for the milk and listening to me gripe. Sorry that I am so crumby tonight. I was just counting on that dried meat for my supper tonight. It will take several days for the meat I have to dry. Don't get me wrong; I am grateful for the milk ya give us. Just I am a big girl now and I need the meat to make me strong. I guess I will just have to learn to get by on less." I rub the goat's neck and give her a hug.

"You're a good girl." Standing up I turn and go back to the cabin and Timmy.

I sit and feed Timmy. Singing to him the way Momma use to sing to me. I lay him on the bed, which he protests. I crawl onto the bed and sit beside him and with a lit candle I start to read from the Bible. At least they didn't destroy or steal it.

After I read a whole chapter, I look down at Timmy who is fast asleep. Smiling I cover him with a cotton cloth and stand up.

"Well; those animals aren't going to clean themselves." I put my hands on my hips, gently rubbing my back as I walk over to the sink. Taking a knife, I begin to remove the head and then gut them. When I have the hides removed, I take the guts outside and dig a hole and bury them.

"Don't need no wild animals smelling these and come looking for a meal." I take the hides to the well, and bring up a bucket of fresh water. I pour the water into the dishpan, from the house, and wash the hides. I must do this over and over until the water remains clear instead of bloody. Then I take the hides back inside and spread them out on the shelf. I get Papa's sharp knife, and begin to scrape the inside of the hides, removing the bloody fatty tissue and a layer of lining. This takes me several hours because I am afraid I will cut through the hides and ruin them.

When I am satisfied they are as clean as they are going to get, I pick up a stone and rub them really hard against the insides, removing the last of the lining. Smiling I go to find Papa's hammer and some nails to nail the hides to the outside barn wall to dry. I remember Papa telling me how it was done when he was a boy and the ways have never changed. I am surprised I remembered. It seems like ages ago he told me that. We were still on the wagon train.

The moon is high in the sky by the time I finish my chores and I am exhausted. I am so tired that I just lie down next to Timmy without combing my hair or washing my face and feet. Sometime during the night he wakes up and cries. I reach over, without opening my tired eyes and pat his back. He lays down and goes back to sleep. I think I need him as much as he needs me.

Just as I am dozing off again I remember the Indians. I dare not sleep tonight. They might return. I make myself get up and go to get Papa's gun. Then I lie down in front of the door. No one is going to be able to come through that door without waking me up first. I have to protect Timmy. He is all I have in this world.

Later that same night, he wakes up crying and I crawl over to the bed and pat his back, only this time he is not willing to go back to sleep. I gently pick him up and lie down on the bed with him but he still frets.

Locking our fingers together, I tell Timmy: "We are family. We are one blood. We will always be together. I am going to take real good care of you and I will teach you all about Papa and Momma and the things they taught me. I promised Momma I would take care of you. A promise is a vow, and I intend to keep that vow. I made it just before she died, right here on this very bed. You don't have to worry, as long as I have a breath left in me, I will be watching over you and keeping you safe." Taking him in the fold of my arms, I kiss his forehead, just like Momma use to do me.

"Now, you go back to sleep, knowing your safe in Sara's arms." I pull him closer to me and hum a tune Momma use to sing to me. It is not long before Timmy breathing is steady and deep. He is sleeping soundly. As I listen to his steady breathing, I drift off to sleep myself. We had a hard day riding Molly all day, we are exhausted and sound sleep is exactly what we both need.

I wake up with a jump the next morning. I don't remember what I was dreaming but it must have scared me. I look around and realize I have overslept. Timmy is still sleeping sound, so I slowly scoot off the bed and put pillows all around him so he doesn't roll off the bed.

I head outside and milk the goat and stake her in another grassy area. I turn Molly loose to eat the grass around the cabin. I don't have to worry about her leaving, since the Indians had her she stays close to where ever I am.

When I come back in I see that Timmy is sitting up in bed. This is the first time he has ever sit up by himself. I get all excited and start acting silly and dancing funny. Timmy laughs, but has no idea what I am clapping and laughing about. I pick him up and change his rag. Then I sit down on the floor and play games with him where I am pretending to bite his feet. He is ticklish and laughs and kicks at me, and I pretend to be growling as I nibble at the bottom of his feet. He loves this.

During Timmy's naptime, I clean the cabin, putting back what the Indians had turned over and dumped all over the floor.

Standing back I take a look at the cabin. I take one section of the cabin at a time and straighten it, until everything is put back where it is suppose to be and the things that are broken are put outside behind the cabin. I don't want Timmy to get hurt or cut himself on broken items.

When Timmy finally wakes up, I pick him up and we go looking for flowers. We find some vines with flowers on them. I pull the vines and then I take them to the cabin. Timmy plays with the vines while I string them across the windows. They look so pretty with their blue and purple flowers. When Timmy goes to sleep, I take some of the vines up the hill and put them on the graves. I sit and talk to Papa and Momma and tell them how we are doing and how much we miss them. Then standing I go back down the hill and to the well. I take out one of the rabbits and take it into the cabin to cook for supper. I pierce it with a stick and start to cook it over the hot coals. A fire would cook it too fast.

Timmy wakes and is playing with his toes. I pick him up and sit him on the floor, but away from the fire. I stay too busy to think about how bad things really are. Timmy doesn't seem to realize that our lives are not what they should be. He just accepts that I am here to take care of him and he is happy about almost everything, especially riding Molly.

I found some string and some rocks and put them on the hearth for when Timmy wakes up in the morning. They will be like new toys for him. Momma showed me how mothers on the wagon train would find things to entertain their babies. She said it helps make them smarter. I want Timmy to be real smart. He is sleeping and my own body is fussing about how hard I have been working. He is use to my playing. Something I don't have much time for it anymore if we are going to survive. I crawl slowly into bed with Timmy and take his finger and make our special sign. I close my eyes and say my prayers but before I can finish I drift off to sleep.

The next morning, I rush to do my chores before Timmy wakes. I am getting faster and now I all but run from the barn to the well or from the well to the house. This gives me more time during the day to play with Timmy. I look over at the bed and see he is rubbing his eyes.

Now that he is awake, I sit him on the floor and place the string and rocks in front of him. He is immediately interested and starts playing with them, giving me a chance to run outside to get him some milk.

When I walk back around the corner of the cabin, Timmy is sitting on the front porch. I stop and look and wonder how he got outside. I take the milk inside, and then return to get him, just in time to see him crawl over after a string the breeze is blowing away. Just when did he learn to crawl? He has been scooting for a week or so but never managed to get anywhere when he got up on his hands and knees. He just rocked back and forth. Now I am going to have to be more careful in how long I can leave him alone. I will also have to block the fireplace hearth so he does not get burned. I will have to look for more dangers today and see that those areas are protected from Timmy, or Timmy from them.

Momma used to say to trust God in all things, so I do. Soon the chores get a lot easier and I am getting faster at getting them done. Timmy is crawling and getting into everything.

Every minute of every day I listen for horses or any signs or sounds that aren't suppose to be there. I am living in fear that they will come back. No matter how much I try to put it behind me, I know they are out there somewhere and may come back for us.

Sometimes I pretend our folks are just outside or have gone to town and will be back any moment. This works and lifts my spirits until I see the hill and the graves and reality rushes back like a break in a dam. Now I try to not to pretend anymore. It hurts too much when I remember.

Timmy and I still go to fetch the animals from the traps and reset them. Our lives are routine now and we seem to be getting along just fine. He is growing like a weed. Which also means he can find more things to get into trouble doing. How on earth did women do this with four or five youngins?

Papa's corn is tall and green and I can see a lot of ears on the stalks now. As I sit on the porch, I wonder when I am suppose to pick all those ears. I have been getting a couple as they get ripe but not the whole field. I also have to ask myself just what am I suppose to do with all that corn? I can feed some to the animals, cook some but when it gets hard, what am I suppose to do? Some I will save for planting next spring, but there must be some way to save the kernels for winter and keep them tender.

The weather is starting to get cooler and Timmy and I have started picking up sticks for fire starter. I know we are going to need stumps and cut up logs for a long lasting fire. The sticks burn too fast and have to be replaced too quickly. I sit on the hearth while Timmy sleeps and make plans, trying to figure in all the problems that can come up with bringing the logs to the cabin. I know I cannot cut down a tree. Back in early fall I convinced myself I could but when I tried I knew I couldn't. Now, I figure I will just have to use the trees that have fallen down already. I can use Molly to help drag them to the cabin.

Next trip to go check traps I will keep my eyes open for fallen logs.

One day when I am in the cornfield and peeling back the skin on the cob, it looks ready. I taste one of the corn pearls and it is sweet. It is time to gather the corn.

When Timmy is sleeping, I walk one row up and pull off all the ears and stack them at the end of the row, then walk back to the cabin, picking the corn going back, stacking the corn at the end of the row. Every day I walk the field, pulling the ears and stacking them at the end of the rows.

Eventually, I have picked all the corn. Now I must move the corn back to the cabin. Taking armloads at a time, I carry the corn back to the cabin and stack it on the same side of the house as the well, right next to the porch. I didn't realize I had so much until I finished stacking it and it is as tall as I am and stretches all the way beyond the kitchen window, almost to the well.

Amazed at how many ears I have picked and carried, I just sit and stare at all that corn. What am I suppose to do with it? Momma had never shown me how to make corn meal. What did she do to save it all winter? Did she fry it or boil it or bake it? I know Molly loves corn because Papa had some he fed the mules on the trip out here from back east. When there was no grass for the horses and mules to graze on, Papa fed them corn. He also fed the chickens corn. I know I will have to shuck it and remove the kernels for feed. Then I will haul it to the barn. I can do this on the porch so I can keep an eye on Timmy while I work. The main thing is I am now going to have to figure out how to cook it for Timmy and me. I am just going to have to try to remember how she made it into meal.

I go out to my stump to think. Trying really hard to remember how Momma did it.

I should be able to remember. How I wish I paid more attention to all the things she did to feed us and take care of us. It sure would make things easier if I had.

Early the next morning, I decide I am just going to have to get started and learn as I go. I head for the barn and fetch Molly. Taking several of Papa's ropes I tie them on the saddle.

Last night I thought all night about how I am going to take care of Timmy this winter. I need a plan and this morning about daylight I came up with one. It is a start at least.

Taking Timmy and lifting him up to the saddle, he grabs a hold of the saddle horn and starts saying "Giddy Up" and bouncing. I have to tell Molly to whoa and climb up behind Timmy. We rarely use the saddle anymore, but today we are going to need it.

I guide Molly up the hill and around the bend, looking for fallen trees. When I find one, I climb down and tie the rope around the log and then tie the other end to the saddle. Next I take another rope and tie it around the log and then tie that end to the other side of Molly and to the saddle horn.

"Ya hang on real tight now Timmy." I take the reins and start to pull Molly forward. It takes a few tries before the log begins to move. Finally, it starts to drag and Molly strains to keep it going and I pull harder on the reins and we start back down the hill and around the bend and then down to the house.

Once there, I untie the ropes and hang them on the saddle and lead Molly back up the hill for another tree log. I know we will need a lot of wood to cook by and keep the cabin warm all winter. What I don't know is just how many of these trees will we need. The way I figure it, we can learn to chop up the trees later. The important thing is to get the trees to the cabin first. One lesson at a time, and I know that God will show me the way as I go. He has taken care of us so far and there is no sense in doubting Him now. Momma always said to keep the faith and right now my faith is all I have to depend on, so I am going to keep it.

Momma and Papa said that God was like a member of our family. We might not see Him but He is always right there with us and knows what we need and provides for us. Well, so far He has been really good taking care of Timmy and me since Momma and Papa died.

Days come and go and there has been no sign of the Indians and Timmy is riding Molly like a big boy.

When we go on these trips, whether it be for trapping or for logs. He holds on to the mane with both hands. When we ride without a saddle and he keeps his face against her neck and mane, his toes digging into her hide, and I keep one hand on his leg as I walk beside the mule. The three of us are making a pretty good team.

At night, after Timmy is fed and put to bed, I sit outside and watch the stars. I know I have to keep the cabin warm this winter and came up with the idea to put the blankets over the window shutters. That not only keeps the cold out but it blocks the light at night from getting out where Indians can see it. I can pile Papa and Momma's clothes on top of the bed and we can sleep under them, this will take the place of the blankets I use on the windows and door.

I look up at the stars and talk to Momma and Papa. I tell them what I did that day and what my plans are for the next day. I hope they are pleased with me, and how well I am taking care of Timmy. I remind Momma I am keeping my vow and I lock my index fingers together. It is our sign, a special sign, and I teach it to Timmy everyday. He is already making it when he takes my index finger.

One morning I wake up to the sound of horse hooves splashing across the creek waters. I jump up and grab Timmy. I open the door to run for the tree but realize we can't make it unseen, so I close the door real quick. Standing there I look around, my mind whirling. I feel trapped. I just knew one day this day would come and I thought I was prepared but now I just can't think what I did to prepare. Then I remember.

Grabbing Timmy I slide him under the bed and stuff clothes in after him to make sure he is good and hid. We have played this game many times over and over so I know he will stay quiet and hidden until I come for him. I run for the fireplace and grab Papa's musket and vow we will not be taken alive. We will go down fighting, turning I look around and find a good spot where I can shoot at the door when it opens and hide behind the bench we sit on at the table. I turn it on its side and duck down below the board. I prop the gun barrel on the wood and take aim. I glance over at the bed and Timmy has his hands over his eyes. He learned to do this when we played peek a boo and now every time I tell him to hide, he hides his eyes. I wonders if he believes that if he can't see anything then no one can see him? I smile and turn back to watch the door. My heart is racing and I can feel my hands shaking but the wood bench will help make my aim steady.

I take a deep breath and let it out slowly. I am ready if they are.

Chapter Seven

At first I only hear a man's voice, then a woman's voice. I come out from my hiding place and tiptoe over to the one of the windows. I peek out through the cracks between the boards and see a man helping a woman down from a wagon. She sure is fussing.

Slowly I open the door, barely looking out, I see the woman coming up the steps starring at me. She has a sour look on her face that makes me not like her right away. She is not soft and nice like a lady should be. She is skinny and has a long nose. Her hair sticks out of her bonnet like lightening struck her and she walks with a heavy step, like she is stomping.

"Where is your father, girl?" She bellows.

"He is with my mother. They are close by." I tell her. Then I tell myself that it is not really lying, they are close by. They are just up the hill, under the tree, and they are together.

"We are the Bastrops. We are on our way to Richmond. Would you be so kind to allow us to water our horses? We would also like to walk around a bit and stretch our legs." Mr. Bastrop speaks with a kind voice and I like him immediately. He has a gentle smile and although he isn't a big man, my first instinct tells me deep inside he has a big heart. His eyes sparkle and they are blue like the sky. His hair is thin on top and he walks with a slight limp, nothing real noticeable though.

"The well is around the corner. My Papa would be pleased if we shared our water with you. Help yourself, the flavor is good and please allow your horses drink their fill." I stuck my hand out just far enough to show them the direction of the well, keeping my left hand on the latch behind me. I didn't want them to know Timmy is in here with me, for some unknown reason, I just didn't trust them.

I notice the man does not bother to unhook the team of horses but leads them around the side of the house, wagon and all. Thinking that is a bit strange, then rethinking it over I figure that it wouldn't be strange if they weren't planning on staying very long. He just didn't want to go to the bother of unhitching and having to hitch them back up again.

Meanwhile, the woman marches right up the steps like she plans on coming right on into our home without an invite.

"I would invite you in but my Momma said to never let strangers into the cabin when she and Papa are not here." I know I am doing what Momma would have wanted me to do if she had been here to tell me, however, until now, she never left me alone.

"We are not strangers. My husband told you we are the Bastrops, of Richmond, Virginia. I am sure your mother would not want you to be rude and keep a tired lady outside. I thought we could have some tea and talk. I have not had another woman to talk to in weeks." Her voice sounds angry and it scares me. Momma never raised her voice and always spoke softly, like reading a poem, Papa always said.

"My mother will have to make that decision. I dare not disobey her wishes."

"This child has no manners. She will not allow me to come in and sit down." She turns toward her husband and places her hands on her hips and looks as if she expects him to make me open the door and let them in.

"Now simmer down, Martha. I am sure the child is doing only what she has been told to do."

The horses are almost through drinking and water is dripping from their mouths when they raise their heads. For just a minute, I see them licking their lips, enjoying the good flavor of the water, and then they drink some more.

Turning he adds: "Thank your father for the water and a chance to walk about. We really must be on our way as soon as the horses are through drinking and have grazed a little. Thank you, child, for your kindness." He tips his hat and turns away.

Before I can breathe a sign of relief though:

"Howard, I want something to drink and to rest a spell. You know how I am when I am tired and need a rest." With her hands still on her hips, she doesn't budge an inch in his direction.

Just when I think things can't get worse, Timmy hears the voices and wants to get up. He starts to cry when I don't come over right away to get him. Now they know there is a baby in the house and my heart feels like it is stuck in my throat.

Quickly, I speak up.

"I am sure Papa will be sorry that he missed you when he is told company stopped by. Please have a safe trip." I turn and step back, giving a quick glance back and to see if the woman is walking back down the steps towards the wagon. I breathe a sign of relief.

"I tell you, Howard, there is something wrong here. What kind of parents go off and leave a small child to take care of a baby? You better look around."

"I looked the place over while the horses were eating a little grass. There is fresh meat and milk in the well. Out back a mule is tied up and a goat is near by. Against the side of the cabin is firewood and another two trees ready for chopping. There is corn, ready to be cooked and another stack drying for corn meal. Her parents must be near by. Now can we please go before we wear out our welcome?" He stands by ready to help her into the wagon.

Just as the door is closing, Timmy lets a big scream. He hates it when he thinks I am outside without him. I rush over and pick him up and hear the woman's voice again. Only this time she is stomping in through the doorway. I look up shocked that she had gotten back so quickly.

"See; Howard. What did I tell you? This cabin has not seen a woman's touch in a long time." Turning towards me she puts a hand on her hip and sticks out the other one towards me, pointing her index finger.

"Girl, tell me where are your parents?" She demands, shaking her finger at Timmy and me.

"They are not far away. My folks will give me a lickin if they find ya in here." I am frightened and my voice quivers.

"Howard, see how her voice quivers? Tell her she better tell us the truth."

"We have over stayed our welcome and need to get on down the road before dark. Now go and get in the wagon and we will be on our way."

"I am not going anywhere until her folks come home." She marches over and sits down on the bench at the table.

I give Mr. Bastrop a look begging him to take his wife and go; but he knows she will not leave and he also realizes something is not right. I can see it on his face.

"She will be all right once she has some tea, and catches her breath. Why don't we take a walk outside and let her get some rest." He notices the water heating on the coals, in the fireplace.

I didn't see where I have any choice. There is nothing I can do but follow him out into the yard, with Timmy in my arms, holding him close to me.

Mrs. Bastrop has taken a box of tea off the shelf and is holding it in her hand.

As we walk away from the porch and around the side of the cabin, he talks to me.

"Now, before you say anything, let me talk for a minute, honey. There is meat in the well, but only enough to last another week or two. If your father were around he would have stored enough meat to make it through the winter. The firewood is dry. It will burn fast and hot but will not last for very long. You need green wood to make the coals last through the night because it burns slow.

Your goat will be going dry soon and by the looks of it she is not going to have another baby. That means the baby will be out of milk before the winter is half over. All that corn is good for now is feed or corn meal. It has dried out and is not fit for cooking or boiling. Finally, up on that hill, I see two graves. I see rocks and flowers on them. If I figure right, that is your folks up there. I am not sure how you buried them. It is a mighty big job for a young girl. You did right by your folks. That looks like gold on their graves. It gives them a luster that shines which makes me believe it is fool's gold.

Now, young lady, I think you have done a fine job, and I think you're about the bravest person I have ever met. The winters are too harsh in Virginia for youngins to survive on their on. This is the first cabin we have seen in at least four days traveling.

The way I figure it, you love that baby enough that you wouldn't have let us get out of sight before you would have come running and telling us the whole story. I wasn't about to leave you two out here alone, either. Now, I understand how you want to stay near your folks and all, but how would your folks feel about you staying all winter here alone? What would they want you to do?" He gently puts his hand on my shoulder and squeezes gently.

His words are kind and gentle, like Papa's and I know he is right in my heart. I have to protect Timmy and if staying is going to put him in danger then I have to go. I sure don't want to leave this place and leave my folks behind though.

"My folks are in the graves. I am sorry I misled you, but I have to protect my brother. What about my mule, Molly? My goat? I can't just leave them here to starve to death. All we have is in the cabin. All of my parent's things are in there. Timmy was born there and Papa built it by himself. I just can't walk away and leave it. I thought about it many times but I am too scared of the Indians or that I will get lost or eaten by bears. I know about winters here. We spent last winter here. Your right about the thought of staying here alone scares me. I say prayers to God every day and every night and ask Him to take care of us."

"Did you ever think that maybe God sent us here for you? We will take what we can. What we can't take, we will lock up and someday you can come back for them.

I don't know why I came this way. It is out of my way. Maybe God really did send me for you. I heard about a band of Indians that were causing trouble a while back. They were caught and are now back to living on the land the government gave them. They were just a few hot heads that found a stil and drank too much of that crazy water."

"What about your missus? She didn't seem too happy about us. What will she say?" I didn't care for the idea of telling her about Papa and Momma or the food situation.

"Martha is all talk, sounds rough but once you get to know her you will know there isn't anything to it. She has a heart of gold and is a very kind person. I think she already knows she can't leave you out here. May not know why or how, but knows something is amiss. She can have a stubborn streak a mile wide. Lord only knows she has saved my hide many a time. Shoot, no Indian stands a chance against her if he is brave enough to cross her. I know if you give her a chance you will probably like her. Who knows, you may even grow to love her the way I do."

He puts his arms around Timmy and me, then, gives us a hug. It is the first time since Papa died that I have been hugged. I didn't know how much I have missed it until this moment. I couldn't help it but I break down and start crying.

"We are needing to have someone take care of us. If I did it wrong and my mistake would cost Timmy his life, I could never forgive myself. Nothing must ever separate us, not in life or death." Tears start to fill my eyes and as hard as I try to stop them, they slide down my face. He wraps his arms around me and holds us tight.

Mr. Bastrop takes Timmy in his arms and tells me to get the mule and goat ready to travel. He says he will go in and tell Mrs. Bastrop for me.

Boy, I sure am relieved that we will be safe now and not have to worry about Indians or starving to death, and especially that I don't have to be in the house when he tells his wife. I still hold some fear of that woman for some reason.

Walking around the corner, a good feeling of relief comes over me. I look up at the graves and realize this is our only chance. I am still keeping my vow by taking care of Timmy and getting us out of here where we will be safe.

Making sure the animals have plenty to eat and drink, I walk them around to the front of the cabin, just in time to see Mrs. Bastrop coming out of the cabin with Timmy in her arms.

"Now child; while Mr. Bastrop is getting the food from the well, I want you to gather up your things and Timmy's. Get an extra quilt to cover up with and then you will sit behind me in the wagon. I will block off some of the chilling wind that is starting to blow in." Her voice, although still stern, also has tenderness to it now. Even her face doesn't look so scary now.

Hurrying into the cabin, I grab Momma's Bible and Papa's knife for Timmy, when he gets older. Grabbing things for Timmy that belonged to our folks. It might mean something to him when he is older. Stuffing items in a wooden box, I look around for anything else we would need. I carefully folded some crocheted dollies, embroidered collars and pillow covers and finally Momma's recipes books and put them in a feed sack, then in the box. Seeing Timmy's wooden crate, I start filling it with as much cloths and rags as it will hold. Rushing here and there, feeling a panic that something would be left behind that we would regret later. I see Momma's quilt she brought over the big waters and I pick it up and wrap it with another old quilt. I carried everything outside and put them in the wagon. One last look, I see another quilt we can cover up with and run back to get it.

Searching every corner, I turn and walk out the door. I want to stay, it is my home, but I made the vow to take care of Timmy and this is what I must do to keep that vow. At least we are leaving together and alive.

One day we will return to claim our land and cabin. I pray it will still be here for us.

I make a quick dash up the hill with Timmy in my arms. The Bastrops didn't say a word or try to stop us. They understood we needed to say goodbye.

Getting up the hill and standing by the graves, I sit Timmy down beside me.

"Papa, Momma, we are leaving now. We will return someday and make this our home again. See, if we don't go, we won't live through the winter. I will keep my vow to you, Momma, and that means we must leave. We will take your memories with us and every day I will tell Timmy about you and how much you loved us. I am sorry we have to go and leave you here. Goodbye."

I pick up Timmy and dash down the hill, I didn't want to keep them waiting nor did I want to cry. The time for crying is over now. We are together and safe.

After climbing into the wagon, I take Timmy in my arms. Mrs. Bastrop climbs up on the wagon bench seat and turns and tucks us in real tight. She has an extra quilt and wraps it around us and makes sure we feel real warm. She smiles down on us, and then turns to face forward. She wraps another quilt around her legs and one around Mr. Bastrop's. Next she puts another quilt over their laps, blocking the wind going under the bench seat and hitting our backs. With her sitting right in front of us, the wind goes over her and we will remain warm and snug.

I actually feel happy for the first time since Papa died. I thought I was happy before but there was always a part of me that was scared. I am not as scared anymore.

I cuddle real close to Timmy and as we ride away, watching the graves and saying my last goodbyes to Momma and Papa one more time. Feeling a sense of loss and deep sadness, I take Timmy's finger and we make our sign.

We are family, we are one blood and as promised I will take care of you and someday we will come back." Timmy looks up at me. He has never known any other area then this land. His eyes are wide with excitement as he looks all around, trying to see everything.

We ride until after dark. Changing my mind about Mrs. Bastrop didn't take long. She really is nice. She is a strong woman like I want to be someday. I even pray they will be our new folks. We sleep under the stars, with her making sure we are safe and warm and have plenty to eat before we go to sleep. It reminds me what it was like to have a mother and to be pampered. It makes me miss Momma something awful.

Although Mrs. Bastrop voice is rough, her hands are gentle and kind and her heart is good. Mr. Bastrop was right, she is a special lady and I misjudged her.

The very first morning the smell of the campfire wakes me up. The meat sizzling in the skillet and the coffee brewing is a smell I will never forget. Reaching over for Timmy, I discover he isn't next to me. Frighten, I crawl out from under the wagon and find him in Mr. Bastrop's lap, eating biscuits and gravy.

"I take care of my brother. I am responsible for him, ME, no one else." I reach down and take him, hugging him against my chest. Then I realize how awfully rude I sounded. He wants back down and to eat more. I sit down next to them.

"I didn't mean to sound ungrateful. It is just that he is all I have left of my family and I promised to take care of him." I am so ashamed of myself. These are good folks, and I am being rude. I hung my head. Holding Timmy tight against my chest, I rub his back with my hand.

"Didn't mean no harm. Just thought you needed a little extra sleep and thought, maybe you have been missing out on sleeping late. A girl needs to be spoiled a little. We never had one of our own. I sure am sorry to have frightened you, child." Mr. Bastrop hands Timmy another bite of biscuit with gravy.

Boy, if that didn't make me feel lower than a snakes belly, I don't know what would. I hang my head in shame.

"Thank you. I am not used to being spoiled. I have lived so long being scared, I guess it will just take a while to get over that." I give him a weak smile but he puts his arm around me and hugs me and my smile turns into one that stretches across my face.

Mrs. Bastrop's cooking melts in my mouth. It has been so long since I have tasted real food that I can't stop eating until I am completely full. Mrs. Bastrop's eyes sparkled every time I ask for some more. I see her eyes and her expression before she looks away. I know that for some reason she doesn't want me to see she has a kindness to her soul.

Trying to make amends for being selfish with Timmy, I tell them they can play with him all they want, while I clean up the dishes and pack everything for the trip. Mrs. Bastrop protest at first but then she gives in and they have a great time making Timmy laugh. Even while I am working, I am smiling and laughing along with them. Timmy is enjoying all the attention. He has never had this much attention.

I help load the stuff back in the wagon with Mrs. Bastrop while Mr. Bastrop plays with Timmy. I think it is a little strange that he doesn't help but then remind myself that not everyone will be like my Papa.

I hear growling and I turn to see Mr. Bastrop crawling on the ground chasing Timmy. Timmy's giggle makes me feel warm inside. Then Mr. Bastrop catches him and pretends to be eating him and Timmy squeals in delight. I know Momma would have never approved of my selfishness but at the same time I know she is looking down on us now, watching Mr. Bastrop playing with Timmy and knows we are truly happy for the first time since Papa died.

Once again we start off in the buckboard. I hold Timmy and we play in the back. Mrs. Bastrop tells us stories about Richmond and how her family came over on a big boat named after some flower.

I tell her how Momma would talk about the great waters. Mr. Bastrop laughs and tells us how he was born in a log cabin, like Timmy, only in Alabama and called us foreigners. Didn't know what it meant but it couldn't have been bad because Mrs. Bastrop laughs and gives him a hug.

SARA'S VOW

After several days of traveling, with playing games in the back when the roads were smooth and holding on for our lives when they were rough, we laughed and sang songs and had a good time just being with each other, sitting around the campfires and starring up at the stars. Mr. Bastrop pointed the pictures the stars made out to me. Said ships uses the stars as maps. He shows me the big dipper and little dipper. He showed me a bear but I couldn't connect the stars right and nothing looked like a bear to me.

It is after dark when Mr. Bastrop finally halts the horses. Timmy is asleep in Mrs. Bastrop's arms and I have fallen asleep, too. Mrs. Bastrop calls me and I sit up and rub my eyes to help open them so I can see better. I look around and see a really big house sitting on a small hill. There is a walk way up to the house. I climb over the side and hold up my hands to take Timmy. I carry him into the house without waking him.

It is a big house with a fine porch that goes all the way around the house. It has two front doors and fancy lights that light up the whole house. I have never seen anything so beautiful.

The furniture is fancy and the curtains are made of lace. The fireplace is made of stones and has a big painting of the Bastrop's when they were young, hanging over it. I sit Timmy in the middle of the floor and go back outside to help unload the buckboard.

Mr. Bastrop builds a fire and puts a metal barrier in front of the hearth so Timmy will not get burned by crawling too close to the fire or sparks might fly out and burn him.

When I come back in, Timmy is asleep in Mr. Bastrop's lap and he is sleeping, also. Mrs. Bastrop tells me to follow her. I gently pick up Timmy but it still wakes Mr. Bastrop.

"It has been a long spell since I have had this much fun playing with a little one. I can tell that we are already really good friends and it will be a pleasure having both of you with us." He reaches over and gives us a hug and kisses me on my forehead, really gentle.

"Yes, we are good friends. We are lucky that you came and saved us. We will be your friends forever. You and Mrs. Bastrop will always hold a special place in our hearts." The words came out of my mouth but they were my mother's words. I sounded just like her.

We go upstairs so I can give Timmy a bath.

When that little chore is done we go back downstairs. Mrs. Bastrop has fixed us something to eat. I notice Mr. Bastrop didn't eat much. I just figured he was really tired from the trip. It is not long before he excuses himself and goes upstairs to bed. Promising to see us in the morning.

Mrs. Bastrop tells me to get our things. I thought she meant for us to go upstairs for bed, but she walks out the front door. So I carry Timmy and the few things I brought in from the buckboard and put them back in the buckboard. I noticed almost everything we had taken in was already in the buckboard.

We ride across town. The buildings aren't fancy like the houses where they live. The buildings are dark and gloomy. We pull up and stop out front of this tall and long building. I see the tall medal fence and a locked gate. My heart starts racing and I can feel myself starting to shake. I don't know why but I am getting scared, so I hold on tightly to Timmy.

The trees made shadows and the breeze made the shadows move across the grass. It looks like there are people behind the trees, hiding in the shadows. I think about the Indians and I want to turn around and run away. I start to shake and my heart beats really fast.

The tall building has lots of windows and it looks like the iron fence goes all the way around the property, like a tall corral with the building in the middle. The fence has pointed spears on the top and I think maybe it is to keep out the Indians. Then I look up at the windows and wonder if it is really meant to keep something or someone in. I don't like the way this place looks at all and I want to leave.

Mrs. Bastrop rings a bell and two people come out towards the gate.

Mrs. Bastrop calls them Sisters. They are dressed in long black dresses and even have their heads covered with a black scarf and a white piece across their foreheads.

I had seen women dressed like this in New York when we got off the boat. I remember I was real short and Papa had to carry me on his shoulders. Momma said they were Godly people. She didn't know what they were called but said I was to be nice to them. That God loves everyone. I heard her tell Papa, later, that they believe they are married to God. Even at that early age I was amazed at this but I didn't ask any questions, I just understood I was to be on my best behavior around them or they would tell God on me.

We go into a room with a dark desk and some hard wooden chairs with no cushions. The woman behind the desk is being called Mother Superior. I listen and hear her call us orphans. I don't really know what it means but I don't think I like being called names by someone who does not know us. Momma always said it was rude to call people names. When she looks at us she looks sad. I don't trust her.

As I listen, I begin to understand that Timmy and I are going to stay here. Mrs. Bastrop tells her that we are to be kept together. Mother Superior stands up and takes Timmy off my lap. Now I am really scared and I jump up and grab him back.

"He is my brother. He stays with me, No one else. I made a vow on my mother's deathbed that I would take care of him. He ain't no bother." My hands curl up into fists.

Mrs. Bastrop speaks up. "The children are to be kept together, understand?"

She smiles down at me and hands Timmy back to me. Maybe this place will not be so bad. However, I would rather stay with the Bastrops, it is more like a home.

She opens the door and waves us out. I look back at Mrs. Bastrop and I see tears forming in her eyes. She really doesn't want to leave us here but for some reason she is. It just don't make no sense to me. She is a grownup. Grownups can do what ever they want to do.

I feel sorrow for her but my own fears grabs back my attention.

One of the Sisters starts up the stairs, carrying our box, and I follow slowly with Timmy in my arms. The stairs curve to the left and I look way up and I can see another floor with many doors. All the doors are closed. On the walls are pictures of more Sisters and some men dressed in fancy robes with jeweled crosses hanging around their necks. They have hats on but the brims have been cut off. I wonder how they keep the sun off of their faces with hats like that.

Timmy is quiet and is looking at the pictures also. He puts his thumb in his mouth, a sign he is scared, with the other hand he is holding onto my ear, tightly.

I kiss him on the cheek and give him a small hug to reassure him, but to be honest I don't feel safe here. I want to turn and run back down the stairs and out the door, but where would I go? I remember the children that lived on the streets in New York. They begged for food and slept under steps or on the sidewalks. This is not the kind of life I want for Timmy. I promised to take care of him and a roof over our heads is safer than under some steps.

The Sister opens the door to a room and I can see beds with girls asleep. The moonlight is coming through the windows and the room is long with beds lined up on both walls.

At least we won't be the only kids and we won't be alone. I must think only good thoughts. This is what Momma would want me to do.

I step inside and turn and look up at the Sister.

"Find an empty bed for tonight; tomorrow you will learn the routine. If you do what your told we will get along just fine. I warn you, child, there is no place for disobedience. You will be punished if you or your brother can not follow orders." She turns and walks out the door.

Standing there looking at the sleeping girls, I tiptoe to an empty bed and lay Timmy down, wondering what she meant by punishment.

All of a sudden the room comes to life. The girls jump up and surround us, whispering questions from all directions.

"Who are you? What is your name? Is that your brother? How did you get to keep him with you? How old are you? How old is your brother? Where are your parents? Or you an orphan or did your parents bring you here? Do you have any more brothers? Do you have any sisters?

So many questions I don't know where to start. I start laughing. For the first time in a long time we are with other children. We are going to be safe here. The Sisters must love children to have so many and we don't have to worry about wild Indians or bears or freezing this winter.

I start answering the questions when the door fly's open.

"GIRLS! BACK TO BED THIS INSTANT!"

Everyone runs for their bed and jumps in and covers their heads.

"I see you are already starting trouble. I will not have you coming in here and causing havoc among these girls. They need their rest as you do. You will learn that there is a time for everything, and when the moon is high, it is a time for sleeping. You will be getting up before sunrise, I expect you to be dressed and ready for sunrise service. Now to bed with ya, and don't forget to say your prayers. You do know how to pray, don't you?"

"Oh yes Mam. My parents taught me to pray and I am teaching my brother."

"Good. Remember to set a good example for the girls, as well as your brother."

The Sister spins around and walks out the door, closing it softly and quietly.

I am frightened again. I lay down with Timmy in my arms and hold him tight.

Whispering I say a prayer for both of us.

"Dear God; I don't know what kind of place this is, but it is a safe place for now. I need you to keep an eye on us and keep us together. I didn't see any other boys. I don't know what they do with boys, so help me keep my brother with me. I promised Momma. Give me strength to be the kind of person they want me to be. In Jesus name, I thank you."

Closing my arms around Timmy, I whisper to him and then hum a tune to put him to sleep. As soon as I can hear him deep breathing, I stop and close my eyes to go to sleep myself.

The bed is soft and feels comfortable. For the first time, in a long time, I can close my eyes and not worry about Indians breaking down the door. We are going to bed with a full stomach and the one thing that makes me feel better about this is that other children surround us. I am looking forward to meeting the other girls in the morning. I have never seen so many girls in one place. As I feel my eyelids getting heavier I wonder about where are the boys and will Timmy have boys to play with in the morning.

Chapter Eight

Just as I feel sleep taking over, I feel the bed moving. I quickly open my eyes and see the girls gathering around me and two are already sitting on my bed. Looking at the girls I first feel a tinge of fright, but it quickly disappears as I see their faces in the moonlight. Who are these girls and why are they standing or sitting around me? I feel Timmy's heavy breathing against my neck and I know he has already in a sound sleep.

"Come and sit with us. We sit in the center of the room and talk every night. We tell about our lives before we came here and what memories we still have. This way we keep our parents and our past lives a part of us so we never forget." A red headed girl grins and offers her hand to help me up. Another girl gently lifts Timmy off my arm then lays him back down without waking him up.

We go to the center of the room and sit in a circle. The moonlight comes in thru the windows and shines on the girls. The girl's hair makes it appear they have halos around their heads. Their clean faces shine from the reflection of the whites gowns they wear. They are either sitting cross-legged or they have their knees drawn up under their gowns and only their toes show under the hem.

"My name is Rebecca, and I am eight. My parents caught the fever and died on the wagon train going west. My brother and I were dropped off here. He is on the boy's side. Sometimes, we are able to see each other when we all walk going to the chapel. We are not allowed to talk but he lets me know he is all right and I let him know I am, too."

"My name is Elizabeth and I am seven. I will be eight soon but I don't remember when. I just know it is in the winter. My mother got sick and my grandmother brought me here to stay until she got better. That was a year ago. I don't know if she is dead or alive. I want to think she is alive but if she is, why doesn't she come and get me? So, I wait and hope she comes and gets me or my grandmother comes for me one day."

They all nod and bow their heads, looking down, some straightening their gowns or covering their toes. A couple of them wipe away the tears that slide down their cheeks, maybe from their own memories, or maybe because they know no one will come for her.

They seem to understand they scared me, so one by one they tell me their names, and how old they are. I begin to relax, and sit up and to listen and learn.

"I am Sara Anderson and this is my brother Timothy Anderson. We live in the mountains in Virginia. My folks have gone to heaven and we were living alone until the Bastrop's came and brought us to this city. Then last night Mrs. Bastrop brought us here. I don't know where we are or what this place is. Any thing you can tell me I would like to hear."

"Your in Richmond, Virginia. This is an orphanage. Not all of us are orphans but for some of us, our parents moved off and left us behind or maybe they were put in jail. Some were just left alone and were living under the boardwalks or under the buildings. This is a lot better place, at least it is warm and we get food to eat."

"Orphans? I have heard that word but I don't remember what it means. Is it bad?"

"Your sure dumb. It means your folks are dead, gone forever, buried with dirt on top of them." The red headed girl, whose hair is one mass of curls, puts her hands on her hips and speaks out. She is taller than the other girls and seems to be in charge; at least when they are alone and the Sisters are not around.

"Are you an orphan?" I ask trying to understand why she would be so angry.

The other girls laugh, and then stop when the red head doubles her fists and threatens to punch them.

"NO. I am no orphan. My parents are going to come back and get me one day soon."

I hear the others snicker and then stop when they see the fists.

"Well, we are orphans. My Momma died right after my brother was born and my Papa was killed by Indians a couple of months later."

"Did you live here in Richmond?" A small dark hair girl with long hair asks.

"No. We lived south in the mountains."

"Who buried them? You have good neighbors or friends to help?" The dark hair girl sits down by me and puts her hand on my shoulder.

"Papa buried our Momma and I buried my Papa."

The girl's gasps and scoots closer to me so they won't miss a single word.

"You buried him? You dug the hole and put him in it and covered him up again?" The dark hair girl doesn't remove her hand, but gently rubs my shoulder.

"Yes. It wasn't easy and I really don't want to talk about it. I am Sara and this is Timmy. What is your name?" I quickly change the subject.

"Oh I am sorry. My name is Judy. I am an orphan, too. My mother was tall with red hair and freckles. She was the most beautiful woman in the world. One day she went to work and never came home. We lived behind the dry goods store. The man who owns the store came and got me and my sister and brought us here." Her voice breaks and she hangs her head down low.

"Her sister fell down the stairs one day when we were at chapel. She left to go to the chamber room and was running back down the stairs when she fell. The doctor said she broke her neck and didn't feel any pain." A girl with yellow hair spoke this time.

"We better get up and hop back in bed in a hurry. We can talk later. It is almost bed check time. Oh and I am Kathy." The red hair girl is obviously in charge.

Early the next morning, someone wakes me up. I sit on the side of the bed as I watch the hustle and bustle of everyone getting dressed.

Everyone goes into the chamber room; each is washing their faces and drying their hands. Then Kathy takes a brush and starts brushing the little ones hair. Some of the others are putting their clothes on and some are helping the younger ones into their clothes. Kathy is giving orders on who needs to be taken care of next.

I hurry and get Timmy ready and then start on getting dressed when the Sister walks in.

"I see everyone is ready to go, except for Sara. Sara, you will learn to hurry up and get ready and not waste time. This time you will be allowed to come down and eat breakfast but if it happens again you will do without breakfast." The Sister turns and walks out of the room with the girls following her in a straight line. I pick up Timmy up in my arms, and then quickly follow at the back of the line.

"I must try to be faster tomorrow. I have to prove I am not a trouble maker." I fuss at myself as I walk down the stairs with everyone else going to the dining room.

I notice as we walk into the dinning room that the tables are lined up, end to end, and chairs are on both sides. Each girl takes a chair and sits quietly. No one says a word. I find a chair and sit Timmy in my lap. He wants to talk and bang on the table but I stop him. He was allowed to play at the table back home but I sense this would not be allowed here. No one is talking. The room is in total silence. The girls sit with their hands folded in their laps. I hold Timmy's arms with my arms wrapped around him. I whisper in his ear to keep him quiet.

A Sister walks in and nods. She opens a Bible and starts to read. When she finishes she says a prayer and the girls say the same prayer with her. I never heard of this prayer so I just sit there and listen. I will ask someone later to teach me the prayer.

A plate of food is put in front of each girl. Only one plate is given to me, so I feed it to Timmy. The girls are given one glass of milk, which I have Timmy drink also. When we are finished; a girl comes by and picks up the plates, another gathers the glasses. Everything is done in complete silence. We stand and pick up our chairs and silently set them back down against the table. Then we turn and march out in silence.

Once we are upstairs, Judy hands me her biscuit.

"I saw you feed your brother your breakfast. We are not allowed to take food from the area, but your going to need to eat or you will not be able to keep up."

"Thank you, Judy. Please don't get yourself into trouble. I will manage." I take a bite of the biscuit and realize I am really hungry. Timmy wants a bite and I share with him.

The Sister comes in and stands there with her hands hidden inside her sleeves. She hides all emotion. I look for some sign of kindness or gentleness in her eyes but see none. Her eyes are cold. I have to wonder what happened to her to make her this way. Maybe, she used to live in a place like this and never knew her family. I feel sad for her.

"Everyone report to your assigned areas. Sara and Timmy will be working in the dining room. Well, lets get going, your wasting sunlight." She stands there watching as the girls leave the room. I quickly pick up Timmy and start to go downstairs, but she stops me.

"If you can not keep up with your chores and take care of this boy, he will be sent to the boys area and live there." She turns and marches out of the room.

"Don't ya worry, I will keep up with my chores and keep ya with me." I whisper to Timmy. Holding him tightly I follow the Sister down the stairs, with my head held high.

We are taken to the dining room and the Sister starts to tell me what I am to do.

"Your to clean the tables and make sure they are spotless. Cleanliness is next to Godliness. Next, you will get the bucket and scrub this floor on your hands and knees. I don't want to see one crumb on this floor. They are to be clean enough to eat off of. If I find any dirt you will be taking your meals off the floor from now on. Do you understand?"

"Yes, Sister. I will see to it that they shine and you can eat off of them."

"Are you trying to anger me? Child, I think you better keep your mouth shut before it feels my hand across it." The Sister stands towering over me, with her face red with anger.

"I am sorry but I do not understand what I said to anger you. I just promised I would clean the floors as you asked." I am on the verge of tears. No one has ever spoken to me so harshly. What did I say wrong?

"I will be back in to check on you. If that boy slows you down one bit, you will find yourself without him to have to care for." She turns and storms out of the room.

I quickly take the bucket and fill it with soapy water and then come back into the dining room and start cleaning the floor on my hands and knees. I wipe wide areas at a time until I have cleaned the entire room. Then I empty the bucket and return with fresh water and another clean rag. This time I get lower to the floor so I can see better and clean a small area at a time. I take a dry rag and wipe it dry. Next I lower myself to eye level and search for anything that might be on the floor. Then I move to the next spot. It takes me until almost noon to have the floor the way the Sister wants it.

Just as I am putting the bucket away, the lady in the kitchen is giving Timmy a cookie. I thank her and then she offers me a cookie. I can hear the girls coming in to eat their noon meal. Timmy and I sit in the kitchen to eat our meals because we didn't have time to clean up so we could eat with the girls.

As soon as the girls leave, I get the bucket and clean the floor again. Timmy is crawling around and I tell him he is helping me by drying the floor. I search every area of the floor and go into the kitchen to empty the bucket when I hear the Sister coming in complaining about Timmy being in the dinning room alone. I rush back in to explain I had just gone into the kitchen to clean the mop bucket and that he has only been alone few minutes.

"If you expect to keep him with you then I expect you to do just that. He is to stay with you." She turns and leaves the room, before I can say a word.

Bound and determine to keep Timmy with me, I take him into the kitchen and sit him under the table while I take a damp cloth to wipe the tables one more time before the night meal.

"Well Sara; you have done a fine job today. The room has never looked better and I couldn't find a speck of dirt or crumb anywhere." Mother Superior speaks softer then the Sisters and has a smile every time I see her.

"I tried my best. My Momma always said a job worth doing is when you do it right. Papa always said if you have a job to do, do your best and so you can be proud of your work."

"I think your parents were very smart. I am sorry their lives ended so soon." She turns and starts asking the kitchen help what she needs to order from the market.

I decide now is the best time to take my break. I pick up Timmy and run upstairs. I would like to bathe him before supper because after supper I must clean the floors and it will so late when I am done, I will wake every one by trying to get him to take a bath. Timmy has lots of ideas and a bath is never one of them.

Once Timmy is bathed and the bath floor mopped and dried, I head back downstairs to eat supper with the girls. After prayers, I start feeding Timmy and eating some of the food myself. The girls whisper softly among themselves and I learn everyone has to work all day.

The Sisters change the work sheet every Monday morning, assigning where each girl will work that week. This way everyone gets to work different jobs so eventually they can go out and work in the public. The only ones who do not leave are the girls who choose to become Sisters. They have to go to a different part of the home grounds to live and learn a new and different way of life.

Once the meal is completed, the girls leave to return to their rooms. I take Timmy into the kitchen and sit him under the worktable and give him a small medicine bottle with a stone in it for him to rattle.

Quickly, I gather my bucket and rags and start to mop the floor again. As I work I start to hum a song that Momma use to sing: The Old Rugged Cross, the first words are: On a hill far away. I stop when I remember on a hill for away lies Papa and Momma. I immediately feel lonely and sad, so I talk to them.

"I know this is not what you wanted for us. I don't like it either. If we had stayed we might not have made it through the winter. Indians could have come and taken us away or killed us. The first chance I get to run away with Timmy; I am going to take it. I will find work outside of this place and make a home for Timmy and me. You will see, you will be proud of me."

I start cleaning as fast as I can, and with the singing, time seems to fly by. I enter the kitchen and find the kitchen women have finished their work and they are playing with Timmy.

He is loving all the attention and is kicking and laughing. When he looks up he says: "Sara".

I pick him up and thank the ladies for their help as I cuddle him close to me. He reaches up and grabs my ear. They laugh and I explain it is something he started that night when the Indians killed Papa and we had to walk back to the cabin. That seems like ages ago, so much has happened since that night. They look sad and just nod in understanding.

I carry Timmy upstairs, change his cloth and lie down next to him so he will go to sleep. Just as I am drifting off to sleep myself, the girls wake me up.

"Come and sit with us. We do this every night before we go to sleep. It helps us get closer to each other, like sisters. Not the kind that wear black but the kind that is family. We would like you to be our sister, too."

Judy sits down next to me. I am already a sitting position. Judy reaches over and hugs me. Kathy, who is not much on hugging, nods her head in agreement.

"We would like to hear about you and Timmy. What was life like living with your folks? Did they beat you? Were you slapped around? All of us have had rough lives. Some worse than others, some better.

Every night we share our thoughts. What we say, we don't repeat, we don't talk about us when we are working or where the Sisters can hear. I hope you feel you can trust us enough to talk with us. The way we see it, we are family now and we have to stick together."

"Maybe this is why God brought you here. To remind those of us who can remember their parents love and to tell the rest of us, that it is possible to love and have a family even for us."

Nancy, a pretty blond with a front tooth missing, smiles and pats the floor for me to sit next to her. I am already sitting on the floor so I just thank her but stay where I am.

"Momma died just a few days after Timmy was born. Papa buried her on a hill, under the same tree that she taught me how to read under. I took over all her duties and it looked like everything was going to be all right." Taking a deep breath, fighting tears back, my voice softens.

The girls scoot in closer to hear every word. My voice is barely above a whisper.

"One day we took Papa his lunch and fresh cool water. It was a warm day and one of the last falls days before winter. The trees were still heavy with leaves and some were turning red and orange, they made a beautiful sight to see. Timmy was learning to crawl and loved to put everything in his mouth, he was always getting into trouble." I repeat my story, right up to the point where we were brought here. No one interrupts me, and no one mentions it is time to get up to go to bed.

Everyone just sat there with the pictures of my story in their heads. Some hung their heads and wiped away tears. Seems no matter how bad their own lives had been, when someone new comes, the new story is worse then theirs, or they are reminded of theirs.

"We were brought up here and put in the room with all of you. I was so frightened. You were all asleep. So I dressed Timmy for bed and got ready myself and crawled into bed with him. Then I started praying to God to keep a close eye on us, especially now, because I didn't know what kind of place this was. Then, you got up and came over to us, each one told me your names and you know the rest. I am glad to be here with you. It sure beats being so scared that you don't dare fall asleep or ya might wake up with a knife at your throat." I smile at the girls. "I am just happy to have children my age to talk to and feel safe."

The girls all nod and smile.

"We want a family and to be loved, too." Mildred speaks up. "I was left on the front door step when I was only four years old. I don't know why my parents didn't want me. I sat there and watched my mother walk away and get in the buggy with my father. He made the horse go and I remember standing up and calling them back. I never saw them again. Since then I have gone to several homes but they always bring me back. I would like to have someone to call Momma."

I crawl over and hug her.

Standing up I look around at the girls, thinking to myself: At least my mother didn't leave us here; I guess one can find something to be grateful for, even in the saddest moments.

"We must all get into bed or we will never get up on time or feel like doing our chores tomorrow." I look around and then back at my sleeping brother and smile.

"I am glad you have come to live with us. Our lives have not been easy and some of us have never known the love you just shared with us. Those who have will now remember that love. I have been here a long time and I don't believe I will ever find a home. I pray that someday I will find a man to love me and we can make our own home and I will take really good care of my children. They will never end up in a place like this." Mildred waves her hand around the room and looks it over. She looks older then everyone else, even me.

"Soon I will be old enough to leave. I will find me a job and a place to live and maybe one day I can have a family of my own. No matter where I go though I will never forget this place and the family I have here." Mildred smiles at everyone timidly.

"Maybe this is why God brought us here. To remind those of a parents love and to tell the rest of us, that it is possible to love and have a family even for us." Judy says as she stands up and dusts off her gown.

SARA'S VOW

The others stand around them, nodding with tears in their eyes. They are hungry for that kind of love, too. It seems to always be just out of their reach, but, someday, they will find it.

They turn and crawl under the covers, some two and three to a bed. Everything is so quiet that I can hear them breathing. Maybe this is why I was brought here. Momma always said that God has a reason for everything. We just have to wait for him to show us what it is.

I scoot closer to Timmy and cuddle up close. Reaching down I gently lift his tiny hand and wrap index fingers with him.

"We are one; we are family. We will always be together. I will see to it, brother." I gently kiss his closed eyes and smile.

"Not a care in the world, I pray your never unhappy." Closing my own eyes I drift off to sleep. I couldn't believe my body was so tired. I worked a lot harder at home.

Chapter Nine

About a month later, right after breakfast, the Sisters come for Mildred. The girls stop what they are doing as she is taken out of the home. Girls began to slip away and spread the word that the Sisters took Mildred away.

When one of them is taken away without adopted parents, it means they are too old to stay so the Sisters find them a job and another place to live. No one gets to say goodbye. The Sisters believe it only upsets the work routine. We should be happy one of us is gone; it opens up more bed space.

We see it as we have just lost another family member and it breaks our hearts. The kitchen workers tell us the next day that Mildred is now working in the dressmaker's shop. She lives above the shop in a little room that was used for storage. She doesn't have to share a bed or her room. She will be able to wear fine clothes, as advertising her work will bring in business. Mildred can sew really well. Now we should be happy she has a nice place to live.

The Sisters thought this would reassure us; instead, it saddens us. Mildred has never been alone before. We worry she feels abandoned again. I try to reassure them that Mildred now has a home of her own and one day she will marry and have a family of her own.

In the evenings, I tell the girls stories of what it is like to live in the wilderness. While I tell the stories they comb the hair of the younger ones, also making sure their nails are clean and trim, and their ears have been washed.

Sometimes, the girls tell stories on how they lived on the streets and stole food to eat. Some lived under saloons or stores and were always in danger of being run over by horses or wagons in the dirt streets. Sometimes there were gunfights and men were killed.

Nancy remembers seeing her father shot down in the streets by gunfighters. Two of the girls never knew their folks. Fanny and Grace lost family on wagon trains going west and had memories of illness taking their family and they were buried along the trail somewhere.

Perhaps the saddest are those left as newborns and never knew anything else but the home. Whatever their stories, I am grateful I knew my family and will be able to tell Timmy how much we were loved. I can tell him about the long boat ride over and what I remember being told of our grandparents in the old country, and how they wouldn't leave their homeland and friends. I have a lot of stories to tell him, because Papa and Momma told them to me over and over.

Mary is a half-breed Indian girl. Her mother is white. The girls tease her because she wets the bed. They make her sleep on the floor. No one wants to share a bed with her. I know she feels shame and I truly feel sorry for her. The floor is hard and cold. It just is not right.

That is until I tell her to sleep with Timmy and me. I make sure she goes to the chamber room before bed and doesn't drink any water after supper. I also promise if I wake up during the night I will wake her up and help her to the chamber room. Timmy is still wearing cloths but soon I will have to start training him.

On the days I have kitchen duty, I am able to give Timmy a few extra cookies, every chance I get. The kitchen help always set aside some for Timmy. When Mary is on kitchen duty, they would give her the cookies and Mary sneaks them up to Timmy. This won a very special place in my heart for Mary.

When I can't finish my work, I get up at night and go downstairs to finish it. I do this to make sure the Sisters don't take Timmy away from me. I wake up Mary and make sure she goes to the chamber room at the same time. This way if Timmy wakes up, Mary will be awake enough to sing him back to sleep. She is going to help me make sure the Sisters won't take Timmy to the boy's side so she keeps my secret.

The work is always done before the Sisters inspect it after their morning prayers.

They must get up very early, for their morning prayers, because they always wake us up for the sunrise service and prayers.

One night Sister Francis catches me working instead of sleeping. Frighten that the Sister will tell, I stare at her, however, Sister Francis puts her finger to her lips and continues making her rounds. I know my secret is safe with Sister Francis and feel a bond forming with her, or maybe I just want to have a bond with another adult female. I have always been around adults instead of children; I miss being treated like a grownup.

It is months before anyone else is adopted. The red headed girl, Kathy, is first to go.

Helping to pack her things, we each tell her what she meant to us. We are taking turns to give her a hug and kiss goodbye. Kathy, not being one for show of affection, except to Timmy, grins and bares it. Kathy has learned since I came to accept some affection and to give some in return. You just never want to make her mad. She can fight better than any grown man. Some of the girls are afraid of her, but I see a softer and gentler Kathy then they see. She is really a very caring person that is funny and makes me laugh. I really don't want to ever say goodbye to her. I hate this adoption business. I am losing another person I care about. I wish I could be hard and just not care, but Kathy is special to me.

"Remember to show your new parents some affection. They are getting you out of here. They deserve your thanks and some affection. It is not going to kill you and eventually you may just like it." I hate to say goodbye, I have had more than my share, saying it too many times already.

As I hug her goodbye, I try not to cry. Kathy hugs back and then backs away.

"I will be watching to see when the rest of you are adopted. I will find you, we are sisters." Kathy glances around the room and puts on a smile. Maybe no one else notices but I can tell the smile is phony. Kathy has a tender side to her that she won't let others see. I can only hope she learns to trust others and lets them see the real Kathy. She is a great person.

Kathy picks up the box of her few belongings, and without turning back, she walks out the door, her head held high.

No one is allowed out of the room when one is leaving. The Sisters say they don't want any show of emotion and crying. This is a joyous occasion and they want only smiles and laughter.

That night the girls sit around in their circle, feeling their loss and some sadness. I decide to tell them another story to get our minds off Kathy's leaving.

"The fireplace would cast an orange light in the room and our faces would get hot if we sat too close. Papa would sit in his chair, carving toys out of wood for the baby that was coming, and Momma would read me stories from the Bible. We were happy just being together. They never talked to me like a child but taught me to talk like I was grown.

Sometimes, no one would talk and I would watch Papa carve or Momma crochet a baby blanket. On some nights they would help me write my letters and make the right sounds. They were teaching me to read. I didn't know these memories would be all Timmy and I would have left of our family.

Someday, when we are adopted, the memories we make here will be all we have left of each other. Cherish these memories and make new memories with new families. Memories are better than books, they go with you wherever you go, and you have the pictures in your mind."

Kissing each girl on the forehead; then tucking them into bed, just like Momma use to do, I start a new tradition for us.

Since Mildred left I step up as their new leader. I feel almost like a mother substitute. I am the only one that can remember what it is like to have a mother who loves them. I want them to have good memories to take with them when they are adopted, even of this place.

As the nights turn cooler, I look for ways to keep everyone warm. The Sisters do not allow any wood to be burned at night. I have everyone sleep closer together and six to a bed. The body heat of each other helps a little but not enough. Next, I have them pile their clothes on top of the beds for extra cover. This makes a difference, and everyone stays warm at night.

I have to get up earlier and put away the clothes before the Sisters come in to wake them for morning worship. Everyone fears the Sisters wrath. Punishment is always harsh.

In the spring, Timmy is starting to walk and causing my work to be constantly interrupted. More and more of my nights are spent finishing my chores. My fears increasing that they will put Timmy on the boy's side worries me something awful and pushes me to try harder.

"Sara; Get Mary packed and dressed. Bring her to Mother Superior's when she is ready." Sister Elizabeth is the most stern of all the Sisters. No one has ever seen her smile. She turns and leaves without giving any hint of where Mary is going.

The girls rush around, trying to help and their excitement of wanting to help fills the air. Emma combs her hair and puts one of her ribbons in it to make it especially pretty. The girls argue over what she is going to wear, when Ruth goes to her box and takes out a dress she has outgrown and gives it to Mary.

Mary, seeing the dress, has never worn anything so pretty, and bows her head and nods a thank you. Ruth, understanding her loss for words, smiles and tells her to put it on so she can see how it fits.

No one mentions that the chances of a halfbreed being adopted is almost impossible, they each have their own fears as to where Mary might be going.

Sister Elizabeth returns as the girls are telling Mary their goodbyes and good wishes. Timmy, somehow, understands she is leaving and clings to her, crying; "No. No go."

Sister Elizabeth grabs Mary's arm and yanks her out the door, slamming the door on her way out. Slamming the door is forbidden. We all stood there and just starred at the door.

Later, Sister Anna Marie comes in and tells the girls that Mary is adopted. Her new father is a merchant and her new mother runs a dress shop and makes fancy dresses for the ladies. No, it is not the same dress shop that Mildred is working for, but the girls might run into each other now and then.

That night, I sit with the girls and tell them how happy Mary is going to be. Pretty fancy dresses and school and lots of love.

When they finally all fall asleep, I sneak downstairs to scrub the kitchen floor. With Mary gone, her chores have been added to my list of chores. Someone has to do them, might as well be me.

The next morning I am cleaning the chamber pots, a chore I hate. By the time the Sisters make their rounds, all the beds are made. The chamber room is clean and smells fresh. I had just lain down, for the first time since yesterday.

"I want the mattresses taken outside and aired. I want all the linens washed and hung outside. Then as soon as they are dry, return them to their proper beds. Windows are to be washed and floors scrubbed spotless." Sister Elizabeth's firm voice left no doubt she expects the orders to be carried out immediately. She leaves the room, and everyone lets out a sign of relief.

Sister Elizabeth tone never shows emotion, except anger. She also never touches anyone, always being very careful not to allow her clothes brush against anyone or anything. No one has ever seen her hands and the girl's joke that she doesn't have any hands.

"She is like a turtle. She hides in her shell and lets no one in. Maybe something really sad happened to her when she was young. Maybe she has never known love. How very sad for her to be that way. We, of all people, should be more understanding. If we had not grown to care about each other we could have grown up to be just like her."

As much as the girls did not want to admit it, I am right. Sister Elizabeth is like a shell, hollow on the inside.

"Sara." Sister Francis steps into the room that I am cleaning.

"I thought you would like to know that Mr. Howard Bastrop passed on to our Lord last night. He was very ill. Seems they had come back to Richmond to find a better doctor. They had been on a trip when he became ill. The doctors couldn't cure him. Mrs. Bastrop sent word that the reason they couldn't keep you was not you or Timmy. Mrs. Bastrop just didn't think it would be good for you to see another love one die. She felt you have seen enough in your young life." She turns quickly and leaves the room, taking all the air in the room out with her.

I gasp for air, and then turn to Timmy. I pick him up and hug him tightly. I say a quick prayer for the Bastrops and then put Timmy back down. I promise myself not to cry but the tears did not listen and flow down my cheeks anyway.

"Timmy, dust those table legs." If only he could clean up as good as he can mess up. My thoughts return to the time we spent with the Bastrops as I work.

He sat on the stump playing with Timmy while we loaded the buckboard. He didn't unhitch the horses to take them to get a drink that first day. He took too many shortcuts. Mrs. Bastrop, as grumpy as she was, waited on him hand and foot. She watched his every move.

Now it all makes sense. It was to make sure he did not overdo. She made everyone go to bed early and get up late. I thought it was just their way. She was making him get his rest. How sad, how very sad for her, she loved him so much. I wonder what she told him when we weren't there the next morning? I could have been some help if she would have only let me. Even in her unhappiness she thought of us.

"God forgive me for thinking only of myself and Timmy."

I carry the dirty linen downstairs to be washed when I see the top of a head of a young girl and think of Mary. When the girl turns and looks up I realize it is Mary. Mary is crying and her new mother is very angry about something and marches into Mother Superior's office and slams the door. Doors are never to be slammed. Mother Superior is going to be very angry with Mary's new mother.

SARA'S VOW

Putting the linens away in the closet, I turn as I hear the door softly open. It is Mary and she is crying. I remember Mary had told me she was taught to never cry when she was young and living with the Indian side of her family. She was taught her life could depend on her being quiet. This, I understand all too well. Going to Mary, I put an arm around her shoulder and we sink to the floor together. She wasn't an Indian to me, she was just Mary, my sister.

"They don't like me no more. I make wet bed. I don't mean to. I forget and drink water before I go to sleep. They no have animal hides but many covers on the beds. The bed soft, like bed of many grasses. I sleep good, but I no wake to go to chamber room. The mother; she is very angry. She says bad and unkind words to me. She said she no want bad girl but wants a good girl and she bring me back here. She said I ruined her mattress. She get mad because I talk strange when I get upset and she tells me I am dumb. Mother Superior say I not tell of my father who is not white." Mary's whole body shakes from her sobbing.

"No, Mary. You are not bad. White man does not always understand. Remember who you are. They took you away from your people and now are trying to make you into something you are not. You may learn our ways but a part of you will always belong to your people. Just as a part of Timmy and me will always belong back at the cabin and mountains where Momma and Papa are buried. I will help you remember not to drink water before you go to sleep. Soon you will remember by yourself and no one will know. One day someone will come and adopt you and will love you for who you are. You will not have to be ashamed anymore." I pull Mary in close to me and hold her tightly, smoothing back her black hair with my hand.

"You are kind and have good heart. Maybe someday you be a Sister. You know the right words to say and the words of the good book. Maybe you will work here and become a Sister." Mary looks up with tears still in her eyes and attempts to smile.

"No. What ever made you think I would want to be a Sister?" I am shocked and push away so I can look Mary in the face.

"You do not have to think about being kind. You just are."

"Yes, God wants us to be kind. My mother taught me many things; she was very kind and gentle. I do not wish to be a Sister. I am not Catholic. I have a different faith, just as your people worship in a different way, so do I. The only sister I want to be is Timmy's, unless you want to be my adopted sister? Would you like that?"

"Yes. Oh YES. My people have this way they make one a blood brother. I do not remember what it is but they are brothers until death. Just like if they had same mother and father. Can we be sisters until death? If you and Timmy are adopted we still be sisters? Promise me." Mary looks up into my eyes pleading.

"I promise you Timmy will be your brother and I will be your sister until death."

We hug and slowly open the door. No one is in the hall so we leave the dark linen closet and go to our room where Timmy is playing with the younger girls.

When the work is completed and before evening prayers, the rest of the girls return to their room and are surprised to see Mary. They gather around each asking the same questions over and over. It is decided that tonight Mary will tell her story, in the darkness of the night. Only Mary will not tell the whole story, the part about wetting the bed is a secret.

The next morning everything returns to normal. Mary is sent to the kitchen after morning prayers and I am washing windows in the dining hall. I finish all the upstairs and start downstairs. It is nice to see out of clean windows. The sun is bright and glistens on the snow covered ground. Even Timmy seems happier. He is singing a song that only he knows the words to. He plays with a ball of string the girls made for him. Each addition of string made the ball a little bigger and Timmy thinks it is a new ball.

Sister Francis tells me, later, the following events as they happened:

Meanwhile, in Mother Superior's office, a young couple is sitting in the hard, straight back chairs across from her desk. Sister Francis stands with her back to the door and her hands neatly tucked away. Her eyes are on the floor and her face is very solemn.

"Sister Francis will get the children for us." Mother Superior nods to Sister Francis, giving the Sister the order silently to get Timmy and another warning look is cast in her direction to remain silent.

As Sister Francis turns to walk out of the room, she hears the woman say:

"As I said earlier, we want a baby boy or a small boy. We just couldn't possibly take on two children."

"They are brother and sister. She does all his care. I—"

Mother Superior is stopped before she can finish what she wants to say. This disrespect does not happen often.

"I will take care of him. I do not need an older sister telling me how to care for my son or undermining what I say." Anger could be heard in her venomous voice.

Mother Superior looks up sharply and Sister Francis walks out of the door.

"If anyone can put that woman in her place, Mother Superior can. She will not separate the two. Surely she wouldn't. Oh LORD, PLEASE do not allow this brother and sister be separated after all they have been through." Sister Francis walks slowly up the stairs. Hoping it is giving Mother Superior time to change their minds about taking Timothy, although her heart fears otherwise.

"Heavenly Father, Please hear my pleas. These children have seen so much hardship; they need to be kept together. Thy will be done."

Entering the dining room Sister Francis watches Sara wiping the window with a clean cloth and talking to Timmy who is sitting by her feet, listening to every word.

"The snow came down and the next morning our Papa goes outside and begins to roll the snow in a big ball." Sara stops long enough to show Timmy how big the snowball was. Then turning back and wiping the window, she continues her story.

"After he made one ball, he made another one and put it on top of the big one. Then he made a smaller one. He put stones in the ball for eyes and a stick for a nose, then he took some of the mud and made a wide-open mouth and it looked like the snowman was laughing. Next he took off his hat and put it on top of the snowman's head. It was the funniest thing I ever saw. I started laughing and our Papa turns around and sees us watching him and he picks up a little bit of snow and makes a small ball and throws it at us. It misses and I run over to him and he takes you out of my arms and spins around with you. You're laughing and it makes Papa laugh. He didn't laugh very much anymore and it was sure good to hear him laugh again. The snowman was this big." Sara turns and raises her hands above her head and stands on her toes. Timmy is watching her, listening to every word.

Sara turns and notices Sister Francis and quickly stands flat-footed again.

"Sorry Sister. I was just telling Timmy about Papa building a snowman. If I keep telling him stories maybe he will feel like he remembers Papa and Momma when he gets big. He won't have any memories if I don't. He is just too small to remember, so I have to remember for both of us."

"Sara. Mother Superior would like for you to take Timothy upstairs and clean up a bit. There is someone in her office that she wishes for you to meet." Well, Timothy anyway. Maybe when they see Sara they will change their minds, Sister Francis is not one to give up on prayer or hope.

"Are we going to be adopted? Are we going to get a family?" The excitement in Sara's voice threatens to tear at Sister Francis's heart. She must not let on.

Sara quickly picks up Timmy and runs up the stairs, causing the other girls to look up and around the corners to see what is going on, giving each other smiles.

Sara's excitement is contagious and the girls wait patiently for the Sister to follow Sara so they can gather and talk. Nancy takes off running for the laundry to tell Mary.

SARA'S VOW

Sara gets a rag and wets it to give Timmy what her Momma use to call a spit bath. Only she uses water. It is not a real bath, more like a wipe off and go type bath. The whole time she is telling him how excited she is that they might be adopted. She also tells him that he needs to behave himself and let them see his sweet smile.

In her excitement she did not notice the worry lines in Sister Francis's forehead.

Sister Francis slowly, reverently follows Timmy and Sara around the room with her eyes. Her hands tucked neatly away in her habit.

As soon as Sara has Timmy sitting on the bed in his Sunday best and she starts frantically looking for a dress that will do for her as she talks to Sister Francis.

"I will be ready as soon as I find the dress my mother made me. I am so excited. A family. Oh how I have prayed for this. Not that you haven't been kind, but Timmy needs a home and people to love him. I will be sure he knows all about how nice and kind you all were."

Finding the dress, she slides it over her head, putting her arms thru the sleeves as the dress slides down over her body. She smoothes the material on the skirt and then runs a brush through her hair. Timmy sits quietly, playing with his ball of string.

She turns to Timmy; "Do I look all right?" Timmy giggles and tosses the ball at her. Sara misses the ball and laughs.

As she picks up the ball and hands it back to Timmy, she turns to the Sister.

"If this is all right, I guess we are ready to go." Smiling, she runs over and gives the Sister a big hug. Touching is forbidden and quickly she pulls back and lowers her head.

"Forgive me Sister. I am just so excited and I will say some extra Hail Mary's tonight for it."

Sister Francis is smiling so she knew she was instantly forgiven.

Due to understanding Sara's excitement the Sister nods her head and lets it pass.

"Now, I want you to be on your best behavior. I want these people to see how very special you are. Give them a big smile and don't be scared. They will be our new parents and I will be with you." Bending over, Sara gives Timmy a last minute pep talk.

Picking up Timmy, she takes a quick look around the room and walks out the door.

Going down the stairs she continues to give Timmy advice about being on his best behavior, even though talking is forbidden in the hallways or on the stairs.

Sister Francis knocks on the door and waits for Mother Superior to invite them in.

"This is Sara and her brother Timothy. Sara has cared for Timothy since his birth. Sara is a good cook, sews well, and is the hardest worker we have here. Sara and Timothy share a special bond" Mother Superior is cut off. That is one thing Sister Francis has never seen before, much else twice in one day. She watches as Mother Superior's face turns a crimson red.

"Let me hold him, child." The woman takes Timmy out of Sara's arms without giving her a chance to protest. Turning towards her husband she adds smiling:

"He is just what we want. Look at his dark curly hair like mine, Daniel. Isn't he just perfect? Don't you think so?"

He nods but can't take his eyes off Sara.

Sara blushes and tries to stand up straighter.

She hides her red chapped hands behind her, feeling a little ashamed of them. She then tries to smooth her skirt to hide her knees; they are also chapped from all the scrubbing on her hands and knees.

All the floors are mopped with rags and buckets of lye water every day. Sara worries perhaps they may not want her if she is not pretty enough. All the attention seems to be on Timmy, except for the man who is smiling at her.

Mother Superior takes notice of the potential parents and sees an opportunity.

Money is tight and she has a chance to adopt two of the children to the same family and she is going to do her best to convince them what a help Sara will be.

Sister Francis escorts the two out and shows them the chairs to sit in and wait. Then she returns to Mother Superior's Office for further orders.

"The children came to us last fall. Their mother passed on soon after Timothy's birth. Indians killed their father soon afterwards. Sara is the only family Timothy has ever known. They have a tight bond. They have not been any trouble since they have been here. Sara promised her mother, on her death bed, that she would always take care of Timothy and." Mother Superior's smile vanishes quickly.

"This is all very interesting, but as we have told you we are not interested in adopting a girl. We will take the boy, however. He is just perfect. He will suit our needs just fine." She folds her gloves and gently places them across her lap as an indication that the subject is closed. She never once consults her husband or even looks in his direction. Her mind is made up, and that's it.

"We did not plan to adopt more than one. However; maybe next year we can come back, or sooner maybe, and adopt Sara." Daniel glances towards his wife, pleadingly.

"Don't be silly. We don't need another child. Timothy will have everything and not have to share. Don't give Mother Superior false hope." She turns back to Mother Superior, tilting her head as if daring the Mother to say another word about taking Sara.

Knowing that children are hard to adopt because times are hard in this new land, and also knowing that adopting the two children together was a dream she dared not dream. It is her job to find homes for the children. She has no other choice but give them the boy.

With a deep sign, she turns to Sister Francis, who is standing stiffly at the door.

"Sister, tell Sara to pack Timothy's things. Then lock the door until after meal time." Her jaw is set and her face takes a hard as stone appearance.

Sister Francis knows not to protest. She has to obey. With a heavy heart she opens the door and gently closes it behind her.

Sister Francis goes to the closet and takes out one box.

"Sara, pack all of Timmy's things in this box. I will hold Timmy while you pack."

Hugging Timmy, Sister Francis whispers to him:

"May the Lord be with you and a light on your path, wee one. May the Lord All Mighty forgive us for what we are doing. May you have a good life and may God some day lead Sara back to you. Amen." She crosses her chest and lets out a deep breath.

Aware that Sara is rambling on, Sister Francis tries to listen.

"I really miss having a family, you know. I will miss all of you, of course. The girls, oh, I shall miss them terribly. But a family.oh Sister I am so happy! Timmy really needs to know what it is like to be part of a family. He has no memories of Papa and Momma."

She completes his packing and reaches for a box to pack her things, only to realize there is not one.

Sister Francis sits on the bed and pats it so Sara knows to sit with her.

"Sister Francis, I know you want to say good bye, but it is forbidden to sit on the made beds. I will tell Timmy how special all of you are and."

"Sara. STOP. The people downstairs are here only to adopt Timmy."

"NO. WE ARE FAMILY. ONE BLOOD. WE BELONG TOGETHER. Don't cha understand? We stay together. Tell the Mother No. Please." Sara stands up with her hands made into fists, she is shouting and crying at the same time.

"This has to be my worse nightmare ever," She cries out.

Picking up Timmy, Sister Francis picks up the wooden box and walks out the door, quickly locking it behind her as ordered.

Sara screams and bangs on the door, begging for Sister Francis to open it again and give Timmy back to her.

Never has the Sister heard such terror, much else from a child.

CHAPTER TEN

Sister Francis starts down the stairs, tears streaming down her face, holding Timmy snugly; she whispers her apology in his ear, over and over. She can still hear Sara's screams and demands to bring Timmy back.

Sara keeps yelling Timmy's name and the beating against the door with her fist, shaking the wood that holds it closed. The shear panic in her voice sends shivers down the Sister's spine.

Closing her eyes, once she reaches the bottom, Sister Francis stops for just a moment, pressing Timmy tightly against her chest, she wonders out loud if she will ever be able to get those screams and sounds out of her mind, or forgive herself for taking part in this travesty.

With the opening of her eyes, Sister Francis sees the other girls peering around the corners. Shock is seen on their faces as they realize what is happening.

A shadow catches the Sisters eye. She turns to see Mary crawl around the picture table and rush up the stairs to comfort the now hysterical sister that is tearing out the hearts of everyone that can hear her cries.

Reaching Mother Superior's door, Sister Francis wipes the tears from her face, putting on a stern face, one she did not feel, holding her head high, she opens the door. Slowly walking around the couple to the other side of Mother Superior's desk, she hands Timmy to Mother Superior.

"You may give them the baby, now. They are his new parents."

Mother Superior tries to push Timmy back into Sister Francis's arms but Timmy is lowered to her lap anyway.

"I have done as you commanded. However; I will have nothing more to do with the splitting up of this family," She turns and walks out of the room.

She understands completely that she will be severely punished for her actions. She walks with her head down to the chapel to beg for forgiveness for what they have done. No matter what punishment is inflicted, it will never erase the screams from her mind or her part in destroying what was left of this family.

Mary sits down by the door and tries to comfort Sara. She searches for words but she knows none. In her native language, there are not such words to comfort someone who baby is given away. Although Timmy is not Sara's birth baby, she was the only mother he has ever known. The bond is never to be broken. Mary just cannot understand the white mans ways. Her people would never do such a thing.

Meanwhile, Timmy is put into the arms of his new mother. She coos and talks to him but he looks around, worried that his sister is not there. The adults talk and rub his arm and play with his hands, but his eyes keep searching for her and he keeps pulling his arm away from them. He watches the door and waits for it to open. He pulls his hands away and starts to cry: "Sara. Sara. Come Sara."

"He is just perfect. We will take him. Now we are a completed family. He will never want for anything. We will take good care of him." The woman stands up and nods for her husband to open the door and follow her out.

Mother Superior sits back down, when the door is closed. She had to do it. They have so many mouths to feed. They can't keep them all. He is going to a good home and her job is to find good homes for the children. When she can keep them together she does but in this case, they wanted a baby boy and Timmy was the only one that they had at this time. She tried to talk them into taking Sara but that woman would not listen. She could tell the man was interested. Maybe she should have told them this was the only way they could get Timmy. What if they said they would look elsewhere? She would have to answer to higher ups over that one.

"Sara, they are leaving and taking Timmy with them." Mary almost screams her whispers thru the door.

Sara runs across the room and stares out of the window, trying to get one last look at Timmy. Then she sees them walking down the steps.

"Please take me too. I will be good. Please, Mister, take me too. I will work for you. Please...don't take my brother away from me!! Please take me too! Please, please take me too! We are one blood, Please take me too. Please don't do this."

She beats on the window with her palms against the glass trying to get their attention so hard she just knows the glass will break, maybe then they will hear her pleas.

The man stops and looks back up at her. Sara's face is wet from the tears, and her palms are banging against the windows. He has to hear the panic and pain in her voice.

She holds her breath; a ray of hope engulfs her. She is a pitiful sight she knows.

Sara's palms are plastered against the windowpanes. Her hair is all affray, tears streaking down her face and her cries that could break the hardest of hearts if they heard could only hear her.

The man stops and just looks up at the window. She can see his face.

Sara sees that he realizes that her agony is their fault. He seems to want to go back for her, but his wife is talking to Timmy, all she is interested in is Timmy.

Looking at his wife, then back up at Sara, she can see the pain in his eyes. He looks at his wife then back up at the window again. Why can't his wife see his pain or hear her cries?

As she watches the woman, Sara realizes she is so busy talking to Timmy that she blocks everything else.

Sara looks back to the man and he is still watching her, then he turns and walks away.

Sara makes another vow: "I will never forget you face! I will never forget your face. Do you hear me? I will never ever forget your face!" She screams it over and over.

Sara watches in horror as they get into their buggy and ride away. Her screams are falling on deaf ears. She slumps to the floor. Her world has just crumbled.

Mother Superior comes into the room and Sara hears the anger at her outbursts. She just doesn't care anymore. Timmy is gone, everyone is gone but her.

"Take that child and put her in the closet. She must learn to control herself." Mother Superior turns to Sister Ann and then opens the closet door as she waits for her orders to be carried out.

Sister Ann comes over and gently picks up Sara.

She whispers to her, wanting her to stay quiet and promising she will come back real soon and let her out. Sister Ann is truly a woman of God and has a very gentle spirit. Everyone loves her.

She lays Sara down on the hard floor.

Sara is able to hear the closet door close and then the lock turned. Mother Superior has made sure she will do her time, to think about what a scene she made.

"She is wrong; I am not going to stay. I have nothing to live for anymore."

Feeling very heavy, Sara curls up on the floor.

"Even God did not hear my cries. My heart aches and now I am alone. I just don't care anymore to go on." She whimpers Timmy's name over and over again. Her hair is soaked with tears and clings to her face as if protecting her from further assaults.

Sara calls out for Momma and Papa and can see their faces in the darkness that surrounds her. Her breathing slows and she welcomes the darkness as it blocks out all the light.

"I don't want to see anymore. I want to keep Timmy's face in my mind as long as I can." Just as she drifts off she begins to pray.

"Dear God, take me now. Please let me die. God, they took Timmy! What am I to do now? Please God; take me home. Take me to my Momma and Papa. Let me come home. Forgive me of my sins, Oh Lord, and take me now. I know I am barely seven years old, but I cannot go on anymore, I am tired. I tried my best to take care of Timmy ever since I was six. I did my best and I learned a lot. Now he is gone.

Jesus said let the little children come unto him. God, I am a child. Let me die. Let me come to Jesus. Take me too, God. Take me too."

Somewhere far away is Mary's voice. Mary is calling her, so far away.

She tries to move but her head is too heavy, so she surrenders to the darkness and the peace that sleep offers her.

"Sara. Can you hear me? Sara, it is Mary. Come Sara. Come to Mary. Come to the door, Sara." Mary lays down on the floor and putting her ear to the crack under the door she listens. At first she hears Timmy's name over and over. Then she hears praying. Now she hears nothing.

The girls begin to gather around Mary.

"Can you hear anything? Can you hear Sara? Is she all right?" The girls keep asking the same questions over and over.

Mary lies on the floor, trying to see under the door, just a shadow moving or a sound of a whimper or a foot scrape, but there is nothing.

Mother Superior comes back up the stairs and stops at the door. She sees the fear on their faces and listens and hears no sound coming from the closet.

The girls back away, knowing she will open the door. Some grasp the hands of those standing next to them. Some hold their breath. Some show fear; others have anger on their faces. All of their mouths are stretched tight and frowns on their faces. Not a sound can be heard. They stare as they watch her go to the closet door.

Mother Superior opens the door and immediately the girls all but knock her down as they run to see inside the closet.

Sara is collapsed on the floor. Mary tries to get her to open her eyes, when she doesn't she puts her head against her heart to see if she can hear it beating.

Mother Superior picks Sara up and gently places her on the bed. She turns to Sister Ann and instructs her to go and fetch the doctor right away.

Mary goes around to the other side of the bed and lies across the bed and whispers in Sara's ear.

"Sara, hear my words. I am with you. We will one day find Timmy and get him back. I cannot do this alone; you must stay here with me. You cannot leave and go to be with your mother and father. Timmy needs you here and so do I. Listen to my words, Sara. We need you here. You can not go to the Spirit World."

Mary rubs Sara's arm and then gets a rag wet and folds it across her forehead. She listens to Sara's chest again and then starts talking to her.

There is a great fear that enters Mary's heart. She has seen this happen once in the village and the mother left with the Great Spirit. Mary does not know enough of her people's ways to save Sara. She doesn't remember all the words to the songs that needs singing.

Mary starts chanting, a way for her to pray to drive away the Spirit of Death. She wants to protect Sara, and at the same time questions herself on what she is thinking. She is just a child; she needs a Holy Man. He would know how to save her. Still she keeps chanting, praying she is doing it right. Praying Sara will not leave to live with the Great Spirit.

"Great Spirit, hear my words. Send Sara a spirit animal to protect her. A great animal of great strength and keenness, an animal to guide her back from the darkness, an animal of the darkness that can see through the blackness in her head." She sings in her fathers' language.

"Please Great Spirit do-not take Sara. I plea, with all that is good, that you spare Sara from the darkness. Send her the Spirit Animal." Mary sings this prayer and pleads for her life, the only way she knows how. She has heard the words many times and maybe her English is not very good, but the Great Spirit speaks the language of her people and can see into her heart. The Great Spirit helps those who wish to only help others.

SARA'S VOW

Mary sings her song and chants until she hears footsteps coming up the stairs.

Mother Superior tries to make her stop, but the girls all clap softly with her chant. The words are in some Indian language, and they cannot sing with her, but they can help by supporting her song with keeping the beat.

Doctor McCoy comes into the room and immediately wants to know what happened.

Before Mother Superior can say a word, the girls all say in unison: "Mother Superior gave away her brother. She has no more family. She raised him from birth. Mother Superior just gives him away like he is a puppy or kitten."

Mother Superior starts to say something but Dr. McCoy waves his hand and stops her.

"I understand you have too many mouths to feed. I also understand that you had a choice to keep this family together and you chose not to listen to your heart.

Now, what I see is a young girl who has lost her will to live. This I place the blame on you. I want my instructions followed exactly and don't go and change one word."

"Yes. What do you want me to do?" Mother Superior stands tall and holds her chin up and looks the doctor in the eyes.

"I want this girl here to stay with her day and night. She will take her meals in here with this child and any chores she is suppose to be doing will be done by another.

If Sara opens her eyes I want to know immediately. If she speaks I want to know. If she moves her arms or legs I want to know. You can send one of the Sisters to let me know. I will return." He left no doubt in Mother Superiors mind that he expects his orders to be followed to the letter of every word.

"Now, what is your name?" This time his voice is softer and he looks over at Mary.

"I am now called Mary." She knew he was a doctor and decided he must be an Elder or an important Medicine Man.

"Well, Mary. I think if anyone can get Sara to listen it will be you. I want you to keep talking to her. Try to get some broth in her if you can. If she coughs, stop, and try again later. You're not to be doing any chores or going to chapel or down to eat. Someone will bring your meals to you. Can you stay right here by Sara for me? Can you be my ears and eyes for me?"

"Oh, yes Doctor, I can do this. I wish to do this. I don't want to leave her, I want to make her better." Mary's face showed no sign of pleasure but just concern for her patient.

"If her skin starts getting hot, send for me. Keep a cool rag on her head."

"I can do this." Mary sits down and put her patients hand in her lap, and gently rubs her own hand over the fingers, bending them over her palm.

"I will come back this evening. If there is any change, send for me."

Mary nods she understands but does not take her eyes off her patient.

He then motions for everyone to leave the room, and he closes the door as he walks out himself.

Mother Superior stops on the steps and looks up at the doctor.

"We will know soon if she has lost her will to live. I suggest you go and pray for her." As he takes the bottom step, he turns back for one more look up at the room.

He leaves and returns to his home where his office is also. He takes out his old books and begins to read. There must be something in here that he can do for Sara.

Mother Superior goes to the kitchen and instructs the cooks that Mary will need broth and will be taking her meals upstairs until further notice.

She returns to her office, where she closes the door and locks it. Sitting down behind her desk, her hands cover her cheeks and she begins to cry. Her job demanded she be hard and do what is best for the home as a whole. She could not to get involved with the children

SARA'S VOW

or families if she was going to survive. She never allowed herself to consider what would happen if she made a mistake. She had to be hard, for the children's sake.

Mary begins to sing to a song that her grandmother used to sing to her when she was still with The People. She kept the beat by thumping her hand against Sara's.

When she finished, she starts telling Sara stories that the grandmothers told the children around the fires at night. She describes the valley they lived in and the water falls that ran cool water year around. She whispers in Sara's ear secrets that she learned that white man was never to know. She laughs as she tells her how the boys told some man named Mooney false stories about how they hunted and gathered their food and even wars they had fought, and how when the man and his men left, they would sit around the fires and laugh. Each time he came back the stories got bigger and bigger. Mary laughs and watches to see if Sara smiles.

Grandmother told her laughter was good for the Spirit; it would keep the Spirit from leaving the body. Mary tells her animal stories that should make her laugh. Some of the animal stories taught lessons on how to treat others; others were just funny stories to make people laugh. Mary remembers she use to laugh many times a day, now she does not remember the last time she laughed.

Three days pass and there is no sign of life other than the steady breathing from Sara. Mary never leaves her side longer than to rush to the chamber room and back.

On the fourth day, Mary begins talking about how they will find Timmy and they will take him and leave this area. They will go back and find her tribe and live in peace with them. She describes the valley and the waterfalls and the animals that walk freely in the woods. She tells the meaning of the different animals to their tribe and of the big bird with the white head that flies so high in the sky and does a dance with his mate. He is a sacred eagle and warns her people with a cry when strangers enter their land.

On the fifth day, Mary tells her how the white soldiers came and took the white women away from their families with the tribe. How because her mother was white they took her away from the only family she had ever known. Her father had to be held by a man with a rifle pointed at him, after they beat him for taking a white woman. Her mother did not wish to go but the soldiers made the women go anyway. They tied their hands if they did not have babies. Mary had to almost run to keep up with her mother, whose hands were tied and then the rope tied to the woman in front of her, at the end of the rope it was tied to a horse that a soldier rode.

When the soldiers brought them into town, people starred at them and called the women bad names. Some threw stones at them. This is when her mother left her outside and went into the wood house to talk to the soldiers.

Then men came and picked out their women and some were happy to be back with their husbands, others cried because their husbands took them back but called them names.

Mary remembers watching her mother's husband taking her mother by the hair and sitting her in a chair and yelling words at her that she did not know. He told her mother that she must give the injun child to the Nuns. When she refused he took her himself to the home. Mary believed her mother would come and get her but she never did. At first she was very sad and all she could think about was the kindness she was given by her people and the difference in the way the white people would stare at her and call her names.

Mary also talks about how some of the white people would be kind to her and tell her she was pretty, but they did not want her to come to their homes to live.

She talks about the bears, the elk, deer and cougars. She talks about the big eagles and the mountains, and how the children love swimming in the creeks.

For three days Mary talks to Sara. She carefully spoons broth into Sara's mouth and wipes what spills out. She baths her and combs her hair. She turns her on her side and then again to her back and then on her other side so she would not get sores. Her grandmother taught her this when her grandfather was mauled by a black bear.

The doctor comes every day and checks. Mother Superior comes twice a day. Even the women from the kitchen come when they bring broth or soup and Mary's meals. At night the girls sit around Sara and they share their memories. Mary knows Sara is going to find the strength to come back and she is going to be the first face Sara sees when she opens her eyes. Mary tells her funny stories to make Sara laugh, so her wakening will be a happy thing.

Mary sees Sara's eyes open then close. She scoots closer and talks but the eyes stay closed. Mary sends Nancy to get one of the Sisters, so they can go for the doctor, Mary talks again of going back to the mountains and her people. She tells Sara they will find Timmy and take him with them. Her tribe will welcome anyone she brings to them. Maybe, they can rescue her mother and take her also. Her father will be so happy to see them again.

Mary talks about her grandmother and how she laughs at little things. Her grandfather is an important warrior with the tribe and the men listen to his words of wisdom.

Mary tells how they will climb up the falls, how the rocks are slippery and they have to hang on to branches but once on top, the water is so clear they can see the fish swimming down deep.

Just as Dr. McCoy walks into the room, Sara opens her eyes and looks at Mary.

"Where is Timmy? Did they bring him back?" The words are weak but Mary understands what she is asking. She looks back at Dr. McCoy for help, and he sits down on the bed and tells her about what he has found out.

"They still have Timmy. He will go to the school and play with other boys his age when he is old enough. For now he is getting a lot of attention and lives in a big fine house. He will want for nothing. These people have the money to see to that." He smiles reassuringly.

"He will want his sister. He will want me." Tears form in Sara's eyes and her words are weak, but she gets her message spoken.

"I will not rest until I have my brother back." She smiles at Mary, and sees that Mary understands she heard her words. She closes her eyes and goes back to sleep. Sara needs rest to regain her strength, then, somehow, someway, she plans to escape from this place and take her brother back. This is a vow she makes to herself silently.

It is only a matter of a week or more before Sara is back up and working in the chapel. Mother Superior thought it would be better for her not to be in the kitchen where memories of Timmy would bother her. The work is a lot easier. She dusts off the pews and the kneeling bars and polishes the hard wood floors on her hands and knees. She feels happier doing this because she feels closer to God and she can talk to Him all day while she works.

Doc comes often and then one day he comes and goes into Mother Superior's office.

Sara fears someone is sick on the boy's side and he came to make a report. Instead, she sees Sister Francis taking Mary into the office.

"Is she sick? Did she hide it so well that I couldn't tell?" Sara lies on the floor so as not to be noticed and watches through the doorframe at the office door. It is not long that Mary comes running out of the office and sings out for all to hear:

"I am being adopted! I am being adopted!" She runs upstairs and Sara is fast on her heels. The other girls follow her as they all race up to hear the news and say their goodbyes.

"Mary. Who is adopting you? I didn't see any people go into the office except Doc?" Sara is first to get upstairs and first to speak.

Everyone is saying the same thing. We all keep watch whenever someone comes into the hallway and go into the Mother Superior's office.

"That is who is adopting me! He says I make a good nurse and he needs me to help him with sick people. He will see that I have good food and a place of my own to sleep and I will be paid coins for working. He is a good man and he will be kind to me. He will teach me the healing ways of the white man and maybe someday I can teach my own people some of these ways. I am very happy. Please be happy for me. No white people are ever going to want to adopt me. My mother will never come and get me. This way I might even be able to see her sometimes. She will know I am safe and happy. This is a good thing."

Everyone gives Mary a hug and Karen gives her a ribbon for her hair and a dress is picked out by Lydia from the hand me down box. Soon Mary's hair is brushed and braided and she wears the ribbon and new dress. She looks real nice and everyone says her goodbyes.

Sara stands at the top of the stairs as Mary walks out with her hand in Dr. McCoy's hand.

He looks up and tells everyone they will be seeing her every time he has to come and check up on us. They laugh and wave goodbye.

Although they will miss her, they all know that this is the best thing to happen for her.

That night they sit in the moonlight and tell stories about Mary. They laugh and remember all the good things Mary did for everyone. It is their way of saying goodbye.

True to his word, Mary comes back often and always brings sugar stick candy. She says she buys it with her own money. She helps in the office and sometimes she needs to go to other people's homes and helps. She is learning how to make babies come out of the mother's tummies. She says Doc calls her a midwife. We laugh because she is not married.

One day, Sara is crawling under the pews, dusting the seats underneath when Sister Marie comes in and ask her to follow her. She crawls out and asks if there is something wrong. Sara always has this great fear Timmy will get sick and she won't be there to make him better. At least Mary is seeing him in town and tells me he is happy and healthy.

"No. Mother Superior wishes to see you. Lets go see what she wants."

Sara smoothes her skirt down and dust off her knees. She rakes her fingers through her hair as they walk in the hallway.

Taking a deep breath, Sara watches as Sister Marie pushes the door open. Sara steps in and Sister Marie closes the door but does not come in.

"Now I know I am in trouble" Sara whispers to herself.

"Sit down Sara." Mother Superior does not even look up at her. She is writing something on a paper.

Sara sits down and holds her breath, waiting to find out what her punishment is going to be.

"I have a couple from up north that are interested in adopting an older girl. I think you would be old enough to travel alone. Are you afraid to travel by yourself?"

"No. Thank ya. I have faced a lot of dangers and I ain't scared of many things no more." Sara sits up straight in the chair waiting to hear what comes next.

"I am not scared." She corrects her English.

"Good. If you ain't scared then they must be nice people."

Smiling Mother Superior shakes her head, and rings a bell. Sister Marie opens the door and enters.

"Sister, I want you to get Sara ready to take the next stage north. I understand it will be leaving within the hour. See to it that the kitchen pack her a meal and a canteen."

"Yes Mother." Taking Sara's hand she opens the door and the bell rings again. A signal letting everyone know another child is being adopted.

Sara sees her friends poking their heads around corners and opening doors. As they start upstairs, the others dash up the stairs behind them, knowing they must walk in silence.

As soon as they enter the room, everyone starts talking at once. Sara quickly clean herself up and gets a new dress from the hand me down box. She also puts on a pair of boots because the snow sure does make her feet cold and winter is just around the corner.

They hug and say their goodbyes. Miss Sally meets them at the bottom of the stairs with a package of food wrapped in leather and a string tied around it to keep fresh and from falling out. Sara sees the rest of the kitchen ladies standing at the dinning room door and she waves goodbye to them. One rushes over and sticks an apple in her pocket and kisses her on the cheek.

"I sure am going to miss ya, girl. Go with God." Tears start to form and she quickly wipes them away and gives Sara a big smile.

As they walk out, Sara asks if she could go by the doctor's office to tell Mary goodbye.

"Mary is out at the Myers. Their kids have the poison ivy rash all over their bodies. Seems those boys were wrestling in it. I will tell her the good news."

"I'm sure disappointed but I know how that rash has a powerful itch."

Sister Marie takes her to the stagecoach and helps her in. She briefly hugs her goodbye and hands her a Bible.

"Take this with you and read it everyday. May the Lord be with you." She backs away then adds she will say her goodbyes to Mary for her. She waves goodbye.

"I am being adopted. Wonder if there will be more kids? Wonder if we will live in town or out in the country? Maybe I could have a dog. That would be great. Papa had promised to get me one but never got around to it before he was killed." Her thoughts rush through her mind like a water fall.

Hanging her head down, Sara realizes she is going still further away from Papa and Momma and worse of all Timmy.

As the stagecoach gets ready to pull out a man climbs in and sits across from her.

She smiles but he just frowns.

Sara watches out the window as the horses pull the coach out of town and wonder what the people are going to be like, and will they like her?

As she sees the horses tied up in front of the stores she remembers Timmy and how he loved to ride their mule.

"I will be back for you Timmy. I promise I will be back for you. We will be together again."

She watches the people on the boardwalks, and later the children playing in the school yard. She strains to see if she can see Timmy playing, but the boys are all too old for him.

Turning back she wonders what she would have done if she saw him? Would she jump out and go and take him back? Would she be arrested for it? She tries to memorize every building so when she comes back for him she will remember exactly where the school is. She will be back one day and old enough to take him back.

also available from publishamerica

THE COCKAMAMY WORLD OF A. YOLD

by Paul Mackan

I first met A. Yold in the dumps. I was down there for—well, that's for another time. Two guys meet in the dumps, they're Canadian, they talk! It's a national characteristic. "Strangers in the night?" Not if they're one of us. Now I am one kind of Canadian; Yold is his kind. Anyway, thinking seasonally, I said, "Are you having a happy Easter?"

"Easter-shmeester," he said. "I'm a Jew." It was the start of our friendship.

It felt funny addressing him as "A" all the time, but he wouldn't tell me what name the initial stood for. All he'd say was, "So you should hear it from me; my mother is unorthodox." And after a pause, while I couldn't think of a thing to say, he lowered his head and smiled. "She's the original Hadassa bizarre." And I was in love—do not infer.

Paperback, 81 pages
6" x 9"
ISBN 1-60610-055-6

About the author:

Paul Mackan lives in Ottawa, Ontario. He's an award-winning writer, broadcaster, and film maker. He's the widower of Sara Lee (Harris) Stadelman, to whom he remains single-mindedly committed. He does film and stage work, and is a member of both Alliance of Canadian Television and Radio Artists, and Canadian Actors' Equity.

available to all bookstores nationwide.
www.publishamerica.com

also available from publishamerica
WHY I AM A COUNSELOR
by Anthony A.M. Pearson

Why I Am a Counselor is a powerful and painful story about a little boy's journey into the darkness and what he learned. It is about overcoming, persevering, discovering purpose, and about liberation and success! Inspiring all who have heard it, it is a true story about a spiritual-psychological awakening that brought about an empowered, authentic life. It explores the questions:
• What forces can take a sickly, fearful, abused child and empower him to become a minister, teacher, and counselor of excellence?
• What is a counselor, and what was the journey that led the author to become a counselor?
• What beneficial life lessons can be drawn from the myriads of counseling theories?
• Can a spiritual-psychological collaboration benefit human existence and the counseling profession?
• How do humans reach maximum potential?   The author hopes that this self-revelation will inspire others to make their own journeys, overcome challenges, and understand their purpose in life.

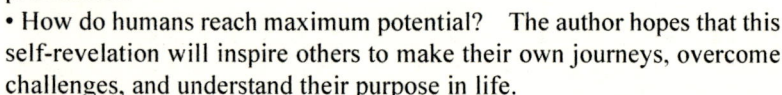

Paperback, 133 pages
5.5" x 8.5"
ISBN 1-4241-9186-6

About the author:

Anthony A.M. Pearson is an ordained minister, educator, counselor, teacher, historian and motivational speaker. He was trained in theology, history, and counseling psychology. He is married, with five sons and nine grandchildren. A recipient of numerous honors and recognitions, he is founder of **Winds of Change Institute**, a human-potential organization.

available to all bookstores nationwide.
www.publishamerica.com

also available from publishamerica
THE 1776 SCROLL
By Louise Harris

Living alone in Philadelphia, 19-year-old Charlie Schofield struggles to repair the shattered relationships in her life while fighting for her spot in the Magical Strike Force Academy. She takes up with a lonely friend who secretly knows that Charlie is in danger. An evil wizard plots against Charlie over powerful magic locked in a scroll. When Charlie cannot open the scroll to release the magic, the wizard hatches a new plan to discredit her in court using more conventional means: she's to prove herself insane and the scroll a hoax. Will Charlie unlock the magic in the scroll before the wizard goes free? Will she prove that she was the victim and not the perpetrator of a crime? Or will the court decide that she is nothing more than an attention-grabbing witch? It is a race against outer forces and inner demons.

Paperback, 104 pages
6" x 9"
ISBN 1-4241-5098-1

About the author:

Louise Harris aspired to write since her youth. She published her first poem at age 12, wrote her first song at age eight, and became an editor. *The 1776 Scroll* is her first novel. Louise lives in Arizona with her husband, three children and two cats. Her heart remains in Philly.

available to all bookstores nationwide.
www.publishamerica.com

also available from publishamerica
THE HEART DONOR
By Nick Wastnage

When a terrorist group linked to al-Qaeda threaten to target London with a nuclear device, three people, with separate agendas, are thrown together in a scary countdown to a world crisis.

Jake Armstrong, investigating an art theft, wants to know who's got his wife's heart. She died after being caught up in a terrorist explosion and he agreed to her heart being donated.

Becky Rackley, an MI5 agent, received a new heart after rheumatic fever rendered her own heart useless. She meets Jake at a party and comes away believing she's the recipient of his wife's heart—as does Jake, but neither have discussed it.

Paperback, 234 pages
6" x 9"
ISBN 1-4241-7878-9

Grigoriy Nabutov, head of the largest Russian organised crime group, plans the heist of a futurist Russian painting. It fails, and he's forced to bargain with Chechen terrorists seeking high-enriched uranium. A world catastrophe looms, London's evacuated and Jake stares death in the face.

About the author:

Nick Wastnage, once a Royal Marine, shot in a skirmish with terrorists in Borneo, was a retailer before becoming a thriller writer. He was born in East Anglia, England, and lives with his wife and family in Buckinghamshire. *The Heart Donor* is his fifth book.

available to all bookstores nationwide.
www.publishamerica.com

also available from publishamerica
LEFT TO DIE
by Roman Garreis

Josh lives a horrific life. Abused, beaten, and betrayed by those who were to love and protect him, he can no longer bear the misery and hits the streets in search of hope, only to find that life on the street offers no reason for hope at all. His only false refuge is to sink deep into one of his delusions, which takes place in an opulent mansion. Inside, a beautiful paradise awaits with seemingly angelic benefactors who supply his physical needs and desires and nurture his intellectual talents—only to find they have turned him into an unwitting instrument of evil and a powerful weapon that misleads others along the path of death and insanity. Captured in this delusion, his mind keeps him between what he was running from and what he ran to, and there amongst the abusers and users, he is left to die as the strain of his inevitable fate from the drugs, prostitution, abuse and decay takes its toll.

Paperback, 142 pages
5.5" x 8.5"
ISBN 1-4241-9301-X

About the author:

Roman Garreis was born in Philadelphia, Pennsylvania, in 1957 and grew up on the South Side. His parents were divorced when he was five years old. His mother had a habit of moving to different neighborhoods which, along with the divorce and the coldness of city street life, left him detached and beaten down. At eighteen years old, Roman left his troubled life behind, and he now spends his time helping others to do the same.

available to all bookstores nationwide.
www.publishamerica.com

also available from publishamerica

GHOSTLY LOVE
A LOVER'S REVENGE
by J. Ferrell

Jacqueline Summersby finds herself stumbling on a house in the small town of Portsmith. A house that has haunted her dreams for as far back as she can remember. Dreams throughout her life that turn out to be glimpses of reality, releasing a hidden power locked deep inside her. A power used to save her most dear and loving friend, from the clutches of an angry spirit that has vowed to seek revenge on her soul. He tricks her with seduction and charm trying to win her heart, only to find that she has unlocked her hidden power putting an end to his wrath of evil.

Paperback, 231 pages
6" x 9"
ISBN 1-4137-9351-7

available to all bookstores nationwide.
www.publishamerica.com

also available from publishamerica
THE HORSEMAN
by Tom Alberti

Tom Blandini is a young rancher from Arizona who travels to El Paso, Texas, to buy four horses for breeding to build up his herd. His troubles begin almost immediately when he does not have enough money left to bring his horses back to Arizona by train. He makes a hasty decision to ride the horses the 300 miles back to his ranch south of Tucson. During the journey he must deal with an outlaw tracking him to kill him and steal his small herd. He also feels the brunt of a vicious storm that scatters his four horses. Tom's troubles turn worse when he encounters the notorious horse thief Chato Rosario and his bloodthirsty partner Blue Dog. His beautiful and impetuous wife Dominique sets out from their ranch with the help of their trusted foreman Rafael to help in her husband's return

Paperback, 185 pages
6" x 9"
ISBN 1-60474-906-7

About the author:

Tom Alberti was born in Chicago but, from an early age dreamed of owning and riding horses. When he was fifteen, his family moved to Phoenix, Arizona. At the time Phoenix was mostly small with an Old West environment. It was here Tom started riding horses and studying Western history.

available to all bookstores nationwide.
www.publishamerica.com

also available from publishamerica
GOD'S MOMENT
by Franklin Howard

God's Moment is a story of possible redemption, like *The Color Purple*. It'll make you laugh, think, and cry. It's a story that many will relate to and enjoy. It's about a beautiful and sexy African-American woman who happens to be an unwed mother. She seems to always choose her own happiness over her children's welfare. She does the unthinkable to her children. We also find out about her family and how they live life in the South during the Jim Crow era. There are a lot of funny and moving anecdotes in this book that will keep you wanting more. Will this woman's priorities change before it's too late or will she continue to only seek her own happiness? You'll want to know how her story ends.

Paperback, 119 pages
5.5" x 8.5"
ISBN 1-60610-371-7

About the author:

The author was born in 1964, in Memphis, Tennessee. He is a lifelong Memphis resident. He has a beautiful and loving wife, Sophia. Together they have two wonderful and extraordinary children, Brittany and Trey. He currently works for the Internal Revenue Service and really likes his job. He is a Christian. He has an exceptional relationship with his Lord and Savior, Jesus Christ. He says Jesus empowered him to write this book.

available to all bookstores nationwide.
www.publishamerica.com